口說
校園生活英文片語會話

◉ 王仁癸 著 ◉

書泉出版社 印行

　　由於目前英文檢定各種考試，都會考到口說能力，但是國內正規學校所用的英文教科書內容，都偏重學術性文章，造成學生口說能力都不強，順帶也影響到聽力理解能力，於是考量國內學生普遍口說能力較差，筆者以口說片語為主，展開場景式的會話，將一些相關的片語集中在一起，讓學生瞭解在哪種場景下會出現哪些片語，熟習口說的單字、句型與回答技巧，加快口說英文學習的捷徑。

這本書的特點有：

一、分類為五大單元，第一單元為校園學習場景片語，第二單元為校園學習業餘場景片語，第三單元為類似片語，第四單元為必備片語，第五單元為常用短語。

二、片語造句強調口說表達能力，能讓讀者輕易用片語來回答與描述，增加口語的味道。

三、以對話方式呈現片語，目的在於學習口說片語與對話技巧。筆者觀察目前臺灣出版的英文片語書，多是使用單獨的句子來呈現片語的使用狀況，欠缺培養讀者美語的思維能力，因此本書採用對話的書寫方式，除了能使讀者覺得生動有趣外，無形中亦可培養美語的思維能力。

四、內容以校園生活為主，有利於學生熟習校園常用溝通會話與句型，可讓學生在學校生活中用英文溝通無礙。

在熟習本書後,將使你的聽力與口說能力有所增進,可應付國內各種大型的英文能力檢定考試。同時書中的單字、片語與句型為美國校園生活常用語言形式,能學習到真正口說英文的正確用法與意義;最後,非常感謝書泉圖書的鼎力相助,讓本書得以順利出版。

王仁癸

PART 目錄 Contents

Contents

目錄

PART

第 **1** 單元

校園學習場景片語

01 學校上課場景
（選課、考試與用功、筆記與作業、論文、
讀書、忙碌、疲勞、教師小主題）

02 住宿場景
（相處、居住小主題）

03 衣服場景

04 飲食場景
（餐廳、飲食評價與付帳小主題）

05 金錢
（有錢、沒錢小主題）

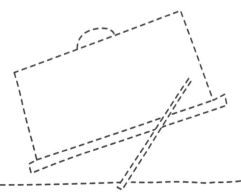

PART

01 學校上課場景

(一) 選課小主題

▶▶ add the course 加選課程

A: I wanted to add this course. And I just found out it is full.

B: Maybe you should check back after the first week to check whether somebody dropped it.

A: 我想要加選這門課程,而我剛剛才知道這課程名額已滿。

B: 或許你應該在一週後再來看看,查看是否有人退選。

▶▶ audit the course 旁聽課程

A: Can I audit the course?

B: You can audit the course for free if you have the instructor's permission.

A : 我可以旁聽這門課程嗎？

B : 如果你得到講師的許可，你可以免費旁聽這門課程。

▶▶ drop the course 退選課程

A : I think I am going to fail the course.

B : You'd better drop the course and retake it next term.

A : 我想這門課我會不及格。

B : 你最好退選這門課程，然後下學期重修它。

▶▶ elective course 選修課程

A : I take Japanese as an elective course next term.

B : I heard it's a very simple and interesting course.

A : 我下學期要選修日文當作一門選修課程。

B : 我聽說日文是很簡單又有趣的課程。

PART

補充

elective course = optional course

▶▶ enlist in 選修

A : I hope I can enlist in a course to learn how to run a company.

B : I think taking business administration is a good choice.

A : 我希望我可以選修一門課,來學習如何經營一家公司。

B : 我想選修商業管理課程是一個不錯的選擇。

▶▶ enroll in 報名參加

A : I'd like to enroll in the seminar in the fall semester.

B : I heard the registration is already over.

A : 我想要報名參加秋季學期的專題討論會。

B : 我聽說報名已經截止了。

▶▶ **major in** 主修

指學習什麼專業。

A : What should I major in if I want to become a merchant?

B : I think majoring in business is a smart choice.

A : 如果我想要成為一位商人，我應該主修什麼？
B : 我想主修商業是聰明的選擇。

▶▶ **register for** 選修

A : I want to register for introductory course and advanced course next semester.

B : You can't take them simultaneously according to the course requirements.

A : 我想要下學期選修初級課程與高級課程。
B : 根據課程要求，你不能同時選修它們。

▶▶ required course 必修課程

A: I'd like to take business ethics as a required course this year.

B: You had better not take it because the professor is very difficult.

A: 我今年想要選修商業倫理當作一門必修課程。

B: 你最好不要選修它，因為教授很難相處。

▶▶ sign up for 選修

A: I want to sign up for the psychology. It's so interesting.

B: I think so. So, I am taking the same class as you are.

A: 我想要選修心理學，它非常有趣。

B: 我也這樣想，所以，我會跟你一樣選修相同的課程。

▶▶ take credit 選修學分

解說

credit 學分。

A : I'd like to take some credits in statistics.

B : Don't you think the course is much too hard for you?

A : 我想要選修統計學某些學分。

B : 你不覺得這門課程對你來說太難了嗎？

▶▶ take over 重修

A : I heard he failed his astronomy course.

B : Right. He has to take it over next term.

A : 我聽說他天文學課程沒通過。

B : 沒錯，他下學期必須重修。

PART

▶▶ transfer credits 轉換學分

A: How can I transfer my credits?

B: It depends on where you are transferring the credits to.

> **A:** 我怎樣才能轉換我的學分呢？
>
> **B:** 那要看你要轉換學分去哪裡。

▶▶ waive a course 免修一門課

A: May I waive a course?

B: Individual courses in the first year cannot be waived according to regulations.

> **A:** 我可以免修一門課嗎？
>
> **B:** 根據規定，第一年的個別課程是不能免修的。

(二) 考試與用功小主題

▶▶ a night owl 夜貓子

A : Are you more of an early bird or a night owl?

B : I'd much rather stay up late, than wake up early.

> **A** : 你比較像是一位早起者，還是一位夜貓子？
> **B** : 我寧願晚睡，也不願早起。

 補 充

I'd rather...than 我寧願…也不願；early bird = morning person；night owl = night person

▶▶ be up all night 整晚沒睡

A : I'll be up all night studying for my exam.

B : There you go again.

> **A** : 我準備考試，整晚沒睡。
> **B** : 你又來這一套。

▶▶ burn the midnight oil 熬夜

指為學習或工作開夜車。

A： The professor said the paper must be sent in before Wednesday.

B： It looks as if I need to burn the midnight oil to finish it.

A： 教授說報告必須在星期三前繳交。

B： 看來我好像必須熬夜來完成報告。

▶▶ cram for 為…苦讀

A： The professor said you don't try to cram for the exam at the last minute.

B： He is right. It only increases your stress.

A： 教授說你們不要在最後一刻才為考試苦讀。

B： 他說得很對，那只會增加你的壓力而已。

exam week 考試週

A: This week is exam week. I only take two exams.

B: I feel like all I have been doing is studying, studying, and more studying.

> A: 這星期是考試週,我只有考兩科。
>
> B: 我覺得我所能做的是學習、學習和更多的學習。

 ## failing grade 不及格

A: Is an F a passing or failing grade?

B: I'm sorry to say that it is indeed a failing grade.

PART

A: F 是及格或不及格呢？

B: 我很遺憾的告訴你，它確實是不及格。

▶▶ fail in the exam 考試不及格

A: I was feeling blue because I failed in the exam.

B: I'm sure it was very difficult.

A: 我心情不好，因為我考試不及格。

B: 我相信它很難。

fail in the exam = fail the exam

▶▶ go over 複習

A: We never went over the chapter 4 in class. Do you think it will be on the midterm?

B: I think it will not be covered on the midterm.

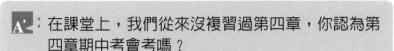

A : 在課堂上，我們從來沒複習過第四章，你認為第四章期中考會考嗎？

B : 我想它不會包括在期中考範圍內。

▶▶ go through 複習

A : Will this chapter be tested?

B : If I were you, I would go through the chapter over and over again.

A : 這一章會考嗎？

B : 如果我是你的話，我會反覆地複習這一章。

▶▶ graduate with honors
以優異成績畢業

A : If I don't graduate with honors, I don't think I could live with myself.

B : I am sure as long as you do well on your Finals, you should be able to meet your goal.

A：如果我沒有以優異成績畢業，我想我會感到內疚。

B：我相信只要你在期末考試考得好，應該就能達到你的目標。

live with oneself 不會感到內疚。

▶▶ passing grade 及格分數

A：I found the exam is too difficult.

B：To be frank, I am looking forward to a passing grade.

A：我覺得這次考試太困難了。

B：老實說，我很期待得到及格分數。

▶▶ pay attention to 專心

A：Bobby goes to class every day, but he still fails in the exam. How is that possible?

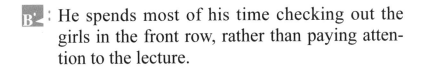

B : He spends most of his time checking out the girls in the front row, rather than paying attention to the lecture.

> **A** : 鮑比每天去上課，但是他考試還是不及格，那怎麼可能呢？
>
> **B** : 他花大多數時間看前排的女孩，而不是專心聽課。

▶▶ perfect grade 優異成績

A : I don't think I've got a perfect grade on the final exam.

B : Well, I must admit the exam was too hard.

> **A** : 我想我沒有在這次期末考得到一個優異成績。
>
> **B** : 嗯，我必須承認，考試太難了。

▶▶ make-up exam 補考

A : I heard you failed the exam.

B : You bet. I will have to take the make-up exam next Wednesday.

A : 我聽說你考試不及格。

B : 沒錯,我下星期三必須要補考。

▶▶ score high in the exam 考試得高分

A : I am happy to score high in the exam.

B : Congratulations. You are likely to be enrolled in the college.

A : 我很高興在這次考試中得了高分。

B : 恭喜你,你很有可能進入大學就讀。

▶▶ stay up 不睡覺

A : I'll stay up all night to finish the term paper.

B : I advise you not to do so, or you will not feel fresh in the morning.

A : 我會整晚不睡覺來完成學期報告。

B : 我勸你不要這樣做,否則你早上會感到精神不好。

▶▶ with flying colors 出色地

指強調非常成功地完成某事。

A: I cannot believe I didn't pass with flying colors.

B: Well, maybe you should have been paid attention in class, rather than played games on your cell phone.

A: 我無法相信我沒有高分通過考試。

B: 嗯，或許你應該上課專心，而不是玩你手機上的遊戲。

(三) 筆記與作業小主題

▶▶ be fit for sth. 適合於

A: Do you think you can help me with my astronomy homework?

B: I don't think I'm fit for that, because I failed that class last semester.

A: 你想你可以協助我做天文學作業嗎？

B: 我想我並不適合，因為我上學期那一科不及格。

補充

be fit for sth. = be fit to do sth.

▶▶ **book report 讀書報告**

A : I have to finish typing up all book reports by tomorrow morning.

B : There goes your sleep tonight.

> **A** : 明天早上之前，我必須打完所有的讀書報告。
>
> **B** : 你今晚沒得睡了。

▶▶ **class work 功課**

A : I have been working on the class work for hours.

B : How about taking a break and going out to eat?

> **A** : 我已經連續寫功課好幾小時了。
>
> **B** : 休息一下到外面吃個東西，你看怎麼樣？

校園中的功課有 homework、studies、class work 與 school work
等說法。

▶▶ drag sb.'s feet 拖拖拉拉

A : I've always wanted to add that information to my paper.

B : You had better not drag your feet on the deadline.

A : 我一直想要增加那些資料到我的報告裡。

B : 你最好不要在最後關頭上拖拖拉拉。

▶▶ hand in 繳交

A : I don't know if I can hand in this paper on time.

B : You can ask if Tom would like to help you.

A : 我不知道我是否可以準時繳交這份報告。

B : 你可以問一下湯姆是否願意幫助你。

▶▶ get backed up （拖拖拉拉）累積

強調忙於某事。

A : In fact, I get so backed up with three papers. They are all due tomorrow.

B : I will miss you at the party tonight.

A : 事實上，我累積了有三份報告待完成，它們全部明天都要繳交。

B : 今晚的宴會上，我遇不到你了。

▶▶ hand out 分發

A : The professor handed out the grade sheets today. He said that you are getting a better grade than the others are.

B : I'm not surprised because I put a lot of time into it.

A : 教授今天分發成績單，他說你會比其他學生得到更好的成績。

B : 我一點也不驚訝，因為我投入很多時間在裡面。

▶▶ jot down 記下

解說
草草記下或匆匆記下。

 A： I always carry a tablet with me to jot down my ideas.

B： That's a good way to keep your ideas. Then you will never forget them.

A： 我總是隨身攜帶平板電腦來記下我的想法。

B： 那真是一個保存想法的好方法，那麼你永遠也不會忘記它們。

▶▶ put it on paper 記在紙上

A： Sophia's speech is excellent and provides me with this valuable opinion.

B： I think so. So I'll put it on paper and read it daily.

A： 蘇菲亞的演講很棒，提供我這個寶貴的觀念。

B： 我也這樣認為，所以我會記在紙上，每天讀它。

▶▶ put off 拖延

A : Have you started working on this paper?

B : In fact, I've been putting it off for days.

A : 你開始寫這份報告了嗎？

B : 事實上，我已經拖延了好幾天。

▶▶ make out 辨認

指看不清楚的時候。

A : I can't make out your handwriting.

B : Sorry, my notes are illegible.

A : 我不能辨認出你的字跡。

B : 抱歉，我的筆記很潦草。

▶▶ take notes 記筆記

A: I often use a notebook to take notes in class.

B: That's a good way to learn. It can record the useful data, so as not to lose them.

> **A**: 我在課堂上經常使用筆記型電腦來記筆記。
>
> **B**: 那真是一個好的學習方法,既可以記下有用的資料,又不會遺失資料。

▶▶ term paper 學期報告

A: My term paper is due tomorrow.

B: It looks as if you will not go to that party to-night.

> **A**: 我的學期報告明天要繳交。
>
> **B**: 看起來你今晚好像不能參加宴會了。

▶▶ term project 學期專題

A: Make sure you don't miss the deadline for the term project again.

B: Don't worry. Tonight I can finish polishing my term project.

A: 你可不要再錯過學期專題的繳交期限。

B: 放心，今晚我就可以潤飾完我的學期專題。

▶▶ turn in 繳交

A: I have to turn in the paper this Friday.

B: The professor said the deadline has been extended for a week.

A: 這星期五我必須繳交報告。

B: 教授說繳交期限已經延後一個星期了。

PART

▶▶ **work on 做**

一般做作業或報告，都是用 work on。

A: I'm going to work on my homework. Be quiet, please.

B: I'm sorry. I will go to another room to listen to music right now.

A: 我正在做功課，請保持安靜。

B: 不好意思，我現在就去別的房間聽音樂。

(四) 論文小主題

▶▶ **be on edge 緊張**

A: Are you feeling OK? You seem a little on edge.

B: I'll be OK. I just didn't sleep that well last night.

A: 你還好嗎？你似乎有點緊張。

B: 我會沒事的，我只是昨晚沒有睡好。

025

▶▶ come up with 提出

解說

指想出或提出計畫、想法。

 : I come up with an idea but I don't know if it is feasible.

 : Why don't you ask Professor White? He is good at Chinese history.

 : 我提出這想法，但是不知道它是否可行。

 : 你為什麼不請教懷特教授呢？他對中國歷史很精通。

▶▶ do a trial run 預演

解說

指做些事情，讓事情可以正常順利進行，也就是「練習」、「試演」或「預演」的意思。

 : Are you free tonight?

 : I have to give a presentation tomorrow and now I need to do a trial run.

> **A**: 你今晚有空嗎？
> **B**: 我明天要做簡報，現在必須進行預演。

do a trial run = give a trial run

▶▶ finishing touches 最後修飾

指報告的最後修改步驟。

> **A**: I am putting the finishing touches on my research paper.
>
> **B**: Sounds great. Soon you can relax and enjoy your life.

> **A**: 我正在為我的研究報告做最後修飾。
> **B**: 聽起來很棒，很快地你就可以放鬆享受生活了。

PART

▶▶ get cold feet 害怕

指在最後時刻，因緊張、害怕或沒信心，而造成手腳冰冷。

A: I am seriously getting cold feet about the presentation on Friday.

B: You only need to speak clearly and confidently.

A: 我是真的很害怕星期五的簡報。

B: 你只需要自信地把話說清楚。

▶▶ give references 註明參考文獻出處

A: The professor pointed out that the paper does not give references in detail.

B: He is right. I need to give references to the sources of information.

A: 教授指出，這篇論文沒有詳細註明參考文獻出處。

B: 他說得很對，我需要註明資訊來源的出處。

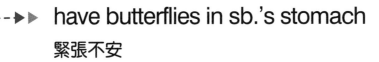
▶▶ have butterflies in sb.'s stomach
緊張不安

A： I am having butterflies in my stomach for today's speech.

B： All I expect from you is to be yourself.

> **A：** 我對於今天上台演講緊張不安。
>
> **B：** 我只期望你表現自然。

▶▶ have trouble 困擾

A： I am having trouble deciding on the topic of research.

B： I think you should choose a topic from the field of study you are interested in.

> **A：** 決定研究主題深深困擾著我。
>
> **B：** 我想你應該從你感興趣的研究領域來選擇主題。

PART

▶▶ like a cat on hot bricks 煩躁不安

A : You're like a cat on hot bricks now. What's the problem?

B : I have to speak in front of everyone for a while.

A : 你現在很煩躁不安，出了什麼問題呢？

B : 我必須在大家面前演講一段時間。

▶▶ look over 檢查

A : Could you help me look over my papers for typos in the lab tomorrow?

B : When would you like me to be there?

A : 明天在研究室裡，你能幫我檢查報告是否有拼寫錯誤嗎？

B : 你想要我什麼時候到那裡呢？

▶▶ narrow down the topic 縮小題目

A: The advisor said my research topic is too broad.

B: He is right, or you will find too much information to go through. Finally, your paper may lack focus and depth. So, you need to narrow down the topic.

A: 指導教授說我的研究主題範圍太廣。

B: 他說得很對,也就是說你會發現資料太多而讀不完,最後你的論文可能缺少焦點與深度,所以你需要縮小題目。

▶▶ on the right track 想法是對的

直譯為「在正確的路上」,在論文寫作情境中,指未離題或方向沒錯。

A: My dissertation needs to give a summary of key arguments in the literature.

B: It seems like you are on the right track to me.

A : 我的論文在文獻上需要歸結一些主要論證。

B : 你的想法似乎是對的。

▶▶ ## time sb.'s presentation
替某人簡報計時

A : The chairperson will time your presentation. Don't worry.

B : Can you tell me what time my presentation is?

A : 主席會替你的簡報計時,不要擔心。

B : 你能告訴我什麼時候換成我簡報嗎?

(五) 讀書小主題

▶▶ ## be absorbed in 全神貫注於

A : She is totally absorbed in the book.

B : It seems like it's hard to tear her away.

A : 她全神貫注於這本書中。

B : 要把她從書中拉走好像很難啊。

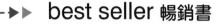

▶▶ best seller 暢銷書

A: I think her new novel will be a best seller.

B: Sure. It's very popular with students now.

> **A**: 我認為她新的小說會是一本暢銷書。
>
> **B**: 沒錯，它現在很受學生的歡迎。

▶▶ detective story 偵探小說

A: I like reading detective stories in my spare time.

B: I love to read, too. But I prefer the social commentary.

> **A**: 在我的空閒時間裡，我喜歡閱讀偵探小說。
>
> **B**: 我也喜歡讀書，但是我較喜歡閱讀社會評論。

PART

▶▶ **fast reader** 看書快的人

A: I'm a fast reader. I can be through with the book in two days.

B: I think I'm a slow reader. I read less than 10 pages in an hour.

A: 我是看書快的人，我可以在兩天內看完這本書。

B: 我想我是看書慢的人，我一小時內讀不到10頁。

▶▶ **get through** 讀完

A: I must get through the book in two days.

B: Are you kidding? The book is pretty thick.

A: 我必須在兩天內讀完這本書。

B: 你在開玩笑嗎？這本書很厚耶。

▶▶ mystery novel 懸疑小說

A : I like reading the mystery novel.

B : Not only you but also I am interested in this type of book.

A : 我喜歡閱讀這本懸疑小說。

B : 不光是你，我也喜歡這類型的書。

▶▶ plough through 鑽研

指必須花費很多精力來閱讀。

A : Every time I see you, you are ploughing through these thick books in the library.

B : I take seven courses this semester. Do you think I have time for parties?

A : 每次我看到你，你都在圖書館裡鑽研這些厚書。

B : 我這學期修了7門課，你認為我有時間參加宴會嗎？

▶▶ pore over 全神貫注地看

解說

常指全神貫注地看、仔細閱讀或深入地思考。

A : Take a break .You've been spending hours poring over your books.

B : I think I should go home and sleep now.

A : 休息一下，你已經花好幾小時全神貫注地看書了。

B : 我想我現在應該回家睡個覺。

▶▶ put down 放下

A : The kind of book is very interesting. Once I start reading it, I simply couldn't put it down.

B : Me, either. I found this book is fascinating.

A : 這類型的書很有趣，一旦我開始閱讀，我簡直放不下來。

B : 我也是，我覺得這類型的書超吸引人。

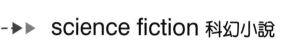

▶▶ science fiction 科幻小說

A：Who can lend me a science fiction?

B：Do you need a little spice in your life?

> **A**：誰可以借我一本科幻小說呢？
>
> **B**：在你的生活中，你需要來點刺激嗎？

▶▶ struggle with 死啃

就是與什麼搏鬥的意思，強調努力地做著某事或者是努力適應某事。

A：I've been struggling with the same chapter for one week.

B：I have a hard time getting through this chapter, too.

> **A**：我一直死啃這相同的章節已經一個星期了。
>
> **B**：我也很辛苦地才讀完這一章節。

▶▶ take an interest in 對⋯感興趣

A : I'm beginning to take an interest in the non-fiction books.

B : It's just the opposite. I like reading the science fictions.

A : 我對非小說類書籍開始感到興趣了。

B : 剛好相反，我喜歡閱讀科幻小說。

▶▶ tear sb. away 將某人拉走

A : Do you think Jane will go to the party with me today?

B : I think it is hard to tear her away from the computer game.

A : 你認為珍今晚會跟我去參加宴會嗎？

B : 我想是很難從電腦遊戲中將她拉走。

(六) 忙碌小主題

▶▶ be in the middle of sth. 正忙於某事

A: Do you want to go out and hang out with me tonight?

B: Sorry, we're in the middle of moving, and the landlord said we need to move out by tomorrow.

A: 你今晚要跟我出去玩嗎？

B: 對不起，我們正忙著搬家，而且房東說，我們必須要在明天前搬出去。

▶▶ be occupied with 忙於

A: I heard Sophia has been studying in the library recently.

B: Well, she is occupied with her dissertation.

A: 我聽說蘇菲亞最近都在圖書館裡用功。

B: 嗯，她正在忙著她的論文。

▶▶ be on a tight schedule 行程很緊湊

A : I have to pick up Jeff from school, then take him to soccer practice, and then go home and cook dinner.

B : I understand that you're on a tight schedule. Maybe we can go out for dinner tomorrow night.

> **A** : 我必須去學校接傑夫,帶他去做足球練習,然後回家煮晚餐。
>
> **B** : 我聽說你行程很緊湊,或許我們明晚可以外出吃晚餐。

▶▶ be overwhelmed with 埋首…之中

A : Angel, would you like to go to the dancing party with me today?

B : I'm afraid not. I am overwhelmed with my biology paper.

> **A** : 安琪兒,你今天願意跟我去參加舞會嗎?
>
> **B** : 恐怕不行,我正埋首於我的生物報告。

▶▶ be swamped with 忙於

A: Could you teach me English?

B: I'm swamped with my papers today. How about tomorrow?

> **A:** 你能教我英文嗎？
>
> **B:** 我今天在忙報告，明天如何呢？

▶▶ be tied up 很忙

A: I will not take that course if I can.

B: You are right, or you will be tied up this semester.

> **A:** 如果可以避免的話，我不會選那門課。
>
> **B:** 你說得很對，否則你這學期會很忙。

PART

▶▶ be up to sb.'s ears 很忙

此片語中的 ears 可用 neck、eyes 或 head 來替代，其意思一樣。

A : So, are you coming over for dinner tonight or not?

B : Here's the deal. I'm up to my ears in work right now, so I'll have to take a rain check.

A : 所以，你今晚會過來吃晚餐或者不會來？

B : 事情是這樣的，我現在很忙，所以必須要改天。

補充

take a rain check 改天。

▶▶ busy bee 忙碌

強調很忙碌且很有效率。

A : I asked Tanya to go to the movies with us, but she is such a busy bee.

B : Well, when you have two jobs and go to school at the same time, you wouldn't have time to go to the movies, either.

A : 我邀坦尼婭跟我們去看電影，但她很忙碌。

B : 嗯，當你有2份工作和同時還要上學時，你也不會有時間去看電影。

▶▶ light schedule 輕鬆的行程

A : Today is a very light schedule, so I can go to Betty's party tonight.

B : Then I will be there on time. See you then.

A : 今天是一個輕鬆的行程，所以我今晚可以參加貝蒂的宴會。

B : 那麼我會準時到達，到時見。

PART

(七) 疲勞小主題

▶▶ a change of pace 改變節奏

強調改變習慣、生活方式等，是為了調劑一下生活。

A: Don't stay in the laboratory all day long. You need a change of pace.

B: I guess so. And I'm looking forward to a fantastic social life.

A: 你不要整天待在實驗室裡，你需要改變一下節奏。

B: 我也這麼想，而我在期待一個多采多姿的社交生活。

▶▶ around the clock 夜以繼日

指連續一整天不鬆懈地做某事。

A: Are you done with the biography?

B: Not yet. Now I first have to study around the clock for my finals.

A: 你讀完這本自傳了嗎？

B: 還沒有，現在我必須先要夜以繼日地準備我的期末考。

▶▶ be beat 累壞

A: How's your classwork going?

B: I think this time I am beat. I have to summarize this book in three pages.

A: 你的功課寫得怎麼樣啦？

B: 我想這次我累壞了，我必須用三頁寫出這本書的大意。

be beat = be bushed = be exhausted = be pooped

be exhausted 累壞

A: I've been studying for four hours.

B: You must be exhausted. You should go out and get some fresh air now.

> **A:** 我已經用功4個小時了。
>
> **B:** 你一定累壞了,你現在應該出去呼吸一下新鮮空氣。

be burned out 累壞

A: I can't stop working on my research plan.

B: Neither can I. I am burned out.

> **A:** 我一直在做我的研究計畫。
>
> **B:** 我也是,我累壞了。

be knocked out 很累

A: I am knocked out. Don't bother me while I am taking a rest.

B：OK. Wait a minute and I will go out.

> **A**：我很累，當我在休息時，不要打擾我。
> **B**：好的，等一下我就會出去。

▶▶ be out of energy 很累

A：I'm working on my thesis day and night.

B：Me, too. I feel I'm out of energy now.

> **A**：我一直日以繼夜地寫我的論文。
> **B**：我也是，我現在覺得很累。

▶▶ be out of steam 很累

A：I'm really out of steam. But I want to watch the documentary at 11p.m. tonight.

B：You had better go to sleep early for your health.

> **A**：我很累，但我想要看今晚11點的紀錄片。
> **B**：為了你的健康，你最好早點去睡覺。

補充

be out of steam = be out of energy

▶▶ put a lot of hours into 投入很多時間

A: I put a lot of hours into writing this article.

B: Don't worry. Soon you will see the great results.

A: 我投入很多時間在寫這篇文章。

B: 不要擔心，你很快就會看到好的結果。

▶▶ stay awake 保持清醒

A: I've been working on the paper since breakfast. Now I feel listless.

B: You should drink coffee to stay awake.

A: 從早餐開始，我就一直在寫這份報告，現在我感到沒有精神。

B: 你應該喝咖啡來保持清醒。

(八) 教師小主題

▶▶ a sense of humor 幽默感

 : It is known that Bill has a sense of humor.

 : Sure. His teaching is so popular with students.

 : 大家都知道比爾很有幽默感。
 : 沒錯,他的教學很受學生歡迎。

▶▶ drop off 睡著

解說
指不知不覺入睡。

 : His lecture is boring. Soon I will drop off to sleep.

 : So I'm really looking forward to break time.

 : 他的演講很無聊,我會很快就睡著。
 : 所以我很期待下課時間的到來。

PART

▶▶ clock watcher 盼下課的學生

A: Don't be a clock watcher. Sometimes you should stay a little after class.

B: I'd like to, but I have to go to work on time.

A: 不要當一個期盼下課的學生,有時你應該下課後多待一下。

B: 我很想,但是我必須準時去上班。

▶▶ doze off 打瞌睡

A: What did you think of the speech yesterday?

B: It was so boring that I dozed off in the middle of it.

A: 你認為昨天的演講怎麼樣呢?

B: 它很無聊,以致於我聽了一半便打瞌睡了。

▶▶ fall asleep 睡著

A : I could hardly keep from falling asleep.

B : Me, too. I can hardly stay awake in his class.

> **A** : 我很難不睡著。
>
> **B** : 我也是一樣,在他的課上,我很難保持清醒。

▶▶ fill sb.'s shoes 取代某人的職位

> shoe 有位置或地位的意思,而取代某人的職位類似說法有 fill sb.'s vacancy、fill sb.'s position、fill sb.'s post。

A : I heard Professor Duke will leave school next month. Do you know who will fill his shoes?

B : I don't know, but nobody can really replace him in school.

> **A** : 我聽說杜克教授下個月要離開學校,你知道誰會取代他的職位嗎?
>
> **B** : 我不知道,但是沒有人能真正取代他的教學地位。

▶▶ finish the class late 晚下課

A : I'm going to finish the class late today, but I guarantee it will be worth it.

B : But I am afraid I will hit a traffic jam when I go home.

> **A :** 今天我會晚下課，但是我保證這是值得的。
>
> **B :** 但是我怕回家會遇到塞車。

▶▶ food for thought 值得深思的事

指精神食糧，提供讓人深思的事。

A : Her lecture gave me plenty of food for thought.

B : I think she gave me a different thought direction.

> **A :** 她的演講提供我許多值得深思的事。
>
> **B :** 我想她給了我一個不同的思考方向。

▶▶ go late 晚下課

A: I'm late, so the class goes late.

B: I'm afraid I have to leave on time to catch the bus.

> **A**: 我遲到，所以全班也晚下課。
> **B**: 恐怕我必須要準時離開去搭公車。

▶▶ on the dot 準時

A: Professor Jack always starts class on the dot, so don't be late.

B: Don't worry. I always arrive 10 minutes early.

> **A**: 傑克教授經常準時開始上課，所以你不要遲到。
> **B**: 不要擔心，我總是提早10分鐘到達。

▶▶ on time 準時

A: Did Professor David come the class on time yesterday?

B: Of course not.

A: 大衛教授昨天有準時來上課嗎?
B: 當然沒有。

▶▶ break time 下課時間

A: She came into my classroom during the break time.

B: What's the matter with you two?

A: 在下課時間,她走進我的教室。
B: 你們兩個出了什麼事呢?

▶▶ run overtime 晚下課

A: My first class is creative writing and it always runs overtime.

B: Then you should often go to the lab class late.

A: 我第一節課是寫作課,總是晚下課。
B: 那麼你上實驗課應該經常遲到。

▶▶ run late 晚下課

A: I hate classes running late, which makes me late to work.

B: Me, too. So I don't like to attend the lab class.

> **A:** 我討厭晚下課，會讓我工作遲到。
> **B:** 我也是一樣，所以我不喜歡上實驗課。

▶▶ thought-provoking 令人深思的

A: Professor Lily has raised a thought-provoking question.

B: You bet. It is worth thinking.

> **A:** 莉莉教授提出了一個令人深思的問題。
> **B:** 沒錯，它很值得深思。

02 住宿場景

(一) 相處小主題

▶▶ be not good with sb. 跟某人處不來

A: Now I need a neat and thoughtful roommate.

B: You don't get along with your current room-mate.

A: 現在我需要一個愛乾淨與體貼的室友。

B: 你是說你跟你的室友處不來。

▶▶ be on good terms with sb.
跟某人處得來

指一切都建立在平等地位上，使得相處關係良好。

A: I'm not on good terms with Mary.

B: Me, neither. I think you need a neat roommate.

A : 我沒有跟瑪麗處得來。

B : 我也是，我想你需要一位愛乾淨的室友。

▶▶ clear the air 消除誤解

A : I have trouble getting along with my room-mate.

B : I think you need to clear the air with your roommate for a pleasant life.

A : 我跟我室友相處有困難。

B : 我想為了讓生活愉快，你需要跟你室友消除誤解。

▶▶ find sb.'s feet 適應新環境

A : I moved on campus last week. I'm trying to find my feet.

B : The dorm life is not terrific. It'll take you some time to get used to it.

A：我上週搬進校內，正在努力適應新環境。

B：宿舍生活不甚精彩，你需要花些時間才能適應。

▶▶ fit into （使）適應

解說

強調到什麼環境都可以適應的很好。

A：I have had a tough time fitting into my new environment.

B：I bet. Moving to a foreign country must be difficult.

A：我在適應新環境上有困難。

B：我同意，遷居到國外一定很不容易。

▶▶ **get along with** 相處得很好

A：I'm getting along with my roommate.

B：I guess your roommate is very thoughtful.

A：我和我的室友相處得很好。

B：我猜你的室友非常體貼。

▶▶ get on well with 相處得很好

A：Unfortunately, I didn't get on well with my roommate.

B：It seems like it is impossible for you two to live together.

A：很不幸，我跟我室友沒有相處得很好。

B：你們兩個好像要在一起生活是不可能的。

▶▶ hit the roof 氣得七竅生煙

A：I am tired of our neighbors blasting their music every night.

B：Me, too. I nearly hit the roof.

A：我厭惡我們鄰居每晚大聲播放音樂。

B：我也是，我氣得幾乎七竅生煙。

PART

▶▶ like cats and dogs 完全合不來

像貓和狗一樣，完全合不來。

A: I heard you are not getting on well with your new roommate.

B: We are like cats and dogs.

A: 我聽說你跟新室友處得不好。
B: 我們完全合不來。

▶▶ make peace with sb. 跟某人和好

A: I would like to move out from my apartment. I'm not getting along with my roommate.

B: You had better make peace with your roommate and I believe eventually she will calm down.

A: 我想要搬離我的公寓，我和室友處不來。
B: 你最好跟你的室友和好，我相信她最後會冷靜下來。

▶▶ put up with 忍受

A : I am finally moving off campus.

B : I can't believe you put up with your roommate for that long time.

> **A** : 我終於要搬出學校了。
>
> **B** : 我無法相信你忍受你的室友那麼久。

▶▶ small talk 閒聊

A : So, what was your conversation with Melanie about?

B : Nothing specific, it was just small talk.

> **A** : 所以,你跟梅勒妮談了什麼?
>
> **B** : 沒什麼特別的,只是閒聊。

small talk = chit-chat

(二) 居住小主題

▶▶ at sixes and sevens 亂七八糟

A : My room is at sixes and sevens after I took the finals.

B : Mine, too. Now I can't find my note books.

A : 期末考後，我的房間亂七八糟。

B : 我的也一樣，現在我找不到我的筆記本。

▶▶ against keeping pets 禁止養寵物

A : I saw the notice that the apartment has laws against keeping pets.

B : I'm afraid that you have to give up keeping your dog.

A : 我看見通知，這間公寓有規定禁止養寵物。

B : 恐怕你必須放棄養狗了。

▶▶ break into 闖入

用強制的手段進入。

A: Someone broke into my home last night and stole my computer.

B: Did the police come over and dust for finger-prints?

A: 昨晚有人闖入我家，偷走我的電腦。

B: 警察有過來採集指紋嗎？

▶▶ close to 離⋯近

A: I'm very lucky. I live very close to campus. I can walk to class.

B: I do envy you. You can save on bus fare.

A: 我很幸運，我住得離學校很近，可以走路去上課。

B: 我真的很羨慕你，你可以節省公車費用。

▶▶ have a sleepover
邀請他人來家裡過夜同歡

常指小孩去同學或朋友家過夜。

A : My mom said I can have a sleepover for my birthday.

B : Cool. This will be a lot of fun.

A : 我媽媽說我可以在生日當天邀請朋友來家裡過夜同歡。

B : 太棒了，那一定很有趣。

▶▶ homely feel 家的感覺

A : Your new apartment has a very homely feel.

B : Thanks. I hired an interior decorator to help me furnish the place.

A : 你的新公寓很有家的感覺。

B : 謝謝，我請了室內設計師來幫我裝潢這住所。

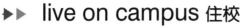
▶▶ live on campus 住校

A : There are many advantages to live on campus.

B : I'll say, So I will live on campus next semester.

A : 住校有很多好處。

B : 你說得很對，所以下學期我會住校。

▶▶ move out 搬出

A : Will you live on campus next semester?

B : Of course not, I'm finding a cheap studio apartment near the school in order to move out of campus.

A : 下學期你會住在校內嗎？

B : 當然不會，我為了要搬出校園，正在學校附近尋找便宜的單間公寓。

▶▶ neat and tidy 乾淨的

A: Your apartment is neat and tidy.

B: I've been at summer camp all week. It's my roommate's doing.

> **A:** 你的公寓很乾淨。
>
> **B:** 我整個星期都在夏令營裡，那是我室友整理的。

▶▶ out of place 很突兀

A: I think the second-hand furniture would be out of place in your house.

B: You can say that again.

> **A:** 我認為這二手家具在你的房子裡看起來很突兀。
>
> **B:** 你說得沒錯。

▶▶ pick up 整理

A : Your house is in such a mess. Don't you ever pick it up?

B : I haven't done any cleaning this week.

A : 你的房間那麼亂，難道你就從來不整理嗎？

B : 我這週還沒有打掃。

▶▶ put sb. up 招待某人留宿

為某人提供過夜地方。

A : I will go to New York and attend a conference next week.

B : That's great. We can put you up for a few days.

A : 下週我要去紐約參加研討會。

B : 太好了，我們可以招待你留宿幾天。

▶▶ room and board fees 食宿費

A: The semester's room and board fees are due next Friday, but I am short of 100 dollars.

B: I would like to lend it to you, but I have no money.

A: 這學期的食宿費下星期五前要交,但是我少100美元。

B: 我很想借你,但是我沒錢。

▶▶ save on 節省

A: Living on campus can save you on bus fare.

B: Yes. But it is cheaper to live off campus than on campus.

A: 住校可以省公車費。

B: 沒錯,但是住校外比住校內便宜。

▶▶ **stay at** 停留在

：What do you plan to do this weekend?

：I think I am just going to stay at home and have a rest.

：這週末你想做什麼呢？

：我想我打算停留在家裡休息一下。

▶▶ **stay put** 不搬

解說

指繼續保持在固定位置或地點上。

：I heard you have trouble looking for a new apartment for next semester.

：So, I decide to stay put.

：我聽說你在尋找下學期的新公寓時遇到了困難。

：所以，我決定不搬了。

▶▶ tidy up 整理

指讓環境保持整潔或整齊。

A: I need to tidy up my apartment now.

B: It looks like your girlfriend is coming to see you again.

A: 我現在需要整理我的公寓。

B: 看來你的女朋友又要來看你了。

▶▶ stay over 過夜

A: I might have to stay over at your house tonight.

B: If you miss the last train, you're welcome to sleep over.

A: 今晚我可能必須在你家過夜。

B: 如果你錯過最後一班火車，歡迎你來過夜。

stay over = sleep over = stay the night

03 衣服場景

▶▶ a good match 很搭配

A : Do you know how to match colors of clothes?

B : I think red and white is a good match.

A : 你知道要如何搭配衣服顏色嗎？
B : 我認為紅色和白色很搭配。

▶▶ be perfect with 很搭配

A : The white shirt is perfect with the dark blue trousers.

B : You are dead right.

A : 白色襯衫和你的深藍色褲子很搭配。
B : 你說得很對。

▶▶ be short of 缺少

A : It seems as if you didn't wash your clothes today. The clothes on the bed were a mess.

B : Yes, I was short of laundry detergent.

A : 看起來你今天沒有洗你的衣服，在床上的衣服很髒。

B : 沒錯，我缺少洗衣粉。

▶▶ blot out 去除

A : I can't blot out the ink stain with soap and water.

B : That's too bad.

A : 我用肥皂和水，不能去除墨漬。

B : 那太糟糕了。

▶▶ dress down 穿著隨便

解說

比平時穿的還隨便，為因應某些場合而必須穿著樸素。

A : I dressed down for my birthday party today.

B : It's better to dress up than dress down.

A : 今天我穿著隨便地參加我的生日宴會。
B : 盛裝打扮比穿著隨便要好。

▶▶ dress up 盛裝打扮

A : Betty dressed up for the party last night.

B : Yeah, she looked so beautiful.

A : 昨晚貝蒂盛裝打扮去參加宴會。
B : 對啊，她看起來好美。

▶▶ dry off 把…弄乾

A: The rain is heavy. I'm so soaked.

B: You had better go to your room to change your clothes and dry off your wet clothes.

> **A**: 雨下很大,我淋溼了。
>
> **B**: 你最好回房間換衣服,把你的溼衣服弄乾。

▶▶ get all dolled up 盛裝打扮

A: Would you mind dressing up for the Thanksgiving party?

B: Not at all. I like getting all dolled up for special occasions.

> **A**: 你介意打扮去參加感恩節宴會嗎?
>
> **B**: 一點也不,我喜歡為特殊的場合盛裝打扮。

▶▶ get out 拿出

A : Fall is over at last. It's time to get out the winter clothes.

B : Sure. Now I have to wear a heavy jacket to stay warm.

> A : 秋天終於結束了,該拿出冬天的衣服了。
>
> B : 沒錯,現在我必須穿厚重的夾克來保暖。

▶▶ go well with 很搭配

A : I think that pink blouse will go well with my skirt.

B : I think you made a good choice.

> A : 我想那件粉紅色上衣很搭配我的裙子。
>
> B : 我想你做了很好的選擇。

▶▶ lose color 褪色

A: The clothes will lose color after washing.

B: That's too bad.

A: 這衣服洗過後會褪色。
B: 那真是太糟糕了。

▶▶ put on 穿上

此片語強調是穿的動作。

A: It's pretty cold outside today. Later, I have to go out.

B: You had better put on your overcoat before you go out.

A: 今天外面天氣相當冷，我等一下必須外出。
B: 你最好穿上你的大衣，再外出。

▶▶ pack up 收拾

A : I am going to my house to pack up some clothes.

B : Where are you traveling to?

A : 我正要回家收拾一些衣服。

B : 你要去哪裡旅行呢?

▶▶ on sale 大拍賣

on sale 必須要以商品為主詞。

A : I heard that the clothes in the store are on sale.

B : That's good news.

A : 我聽說這家店的衣服正在大拍賣。

B : 那真是一個好消息。

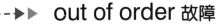

▶▶ out of order 故障

A: The washing machine is out of order.

B: You'd better get it repaired.

> **A:** 洗衣機故障了。
> **B:** 你最好將它送修。

▶▶ run out of 用完

A: What's the matter with you?

B: I ran out of coins during the laundry.

> **A:** 你發生什麼事？
> **B:** 在洗衣時，我用完了硬幣。

▶▶ Sunday best 最好的衣服

A: I need to remind you that tomorrow is Sunday.

B: I know I have to wear my Sunday best to go to church.

A：我要提醒你，明天是星期天。

B：我知道我必須穿上最好的衣服上教堂。

▶▶ take off 脫下

A：Don't you think it is terribly hot today?

B：So, I took off my jacket.

A：你不覺得今天天氣很熱嗎？

B：所以，我已脫下我的夾克了。

▶▶ try on 試穿

A：How do you feel after you try on the new clothes?

B：I feel it's a bit loose.

A：你試穿後覺得這件衣服怎麼樣？

B：我覺得它有點寬。

 飲食場景

(一) 餐廳小主題

▶▶ be booked up 訂光

A: You know the restaurant was booked up several weeks in advance.

B: I know this restaurant is noted for its food.

A: 你知道這家餐廳位子在數週前被訂光了。
B: 我知道這家餐廳是以食物聞名。

▶▶ book a table 預訂座位

A: I want to book a table for two.

B: For what time, sir?

A: 我想要預訂一張2人桌的座位。
B: 先生,要幾點的?

PART

▶▶ come with 附贈

A: I want to order a number two hamburger meal. And what comes with my meal?

B: A bag of fries and a drink.

> **A:** 我想要點一份2號漢堡餐,而我的餐點會附贈什麼呢?
>
> **B:** 一包薯條和一杯飲料。

▶▶ dine out 外出吃飯

A: Let's dine out tonight. I want to try something different.

B: How about seafood?

> **A:** 我們今晚外出吃飯吧,我想要吃點不一樣的東西。
>
> **B:** 吃海鮮如何呢?

▶▶ eat out 外出吃飯

A: Would you like to eat out for dinner with me?

B: I would like to, but I am working on my home-work.

> **A:** 你想要跟我外出吃晚餐嗎？
>
> **B:** 我很樂意，但是我正在寫作業。

▶▶ for here or to go 內用或外帶

A: Is this pizza going to be for here or to go?

B: For here, please.

> **A:** 這比薩是要內用或外帶呢？
>
> **B:** 內用，謝謝。

for here or to go = eat in or to take out

PART

▶▶ go out for lunch 外出吃中餐

A : Let's go out for lunch. I know a good place.

B : It's up to you.

A : 讓我們外出吃中餐吧,我知道一家不錯的餐廳。
B : 一切由你決定。

go out for dinner 外出吃晚餐。

▶▶ house specialty 招牌菜

A : The house specialty is pudding. Do you want to order one?

B : It's a pity that I have no taste for sweet things.

A : 招牌菜是布丁,你要點一份嗎?
B : 可惜我不吃甜的東西。

▶▶ lose sb.'s appetite 失去胃口

指沒有食欲。

A : It's been a long night. Why don't we go and get something to eat?

B : After watching my wife give birth, I think I've lost my appetite.

A : 今夜真漫長,我們為什麼不去外面找點東西吃呢?

B : 在看完我老婆生產後,我想我已經失去胃口了。

▶▶ keep an eye out for sb.
等待某人的來臨

keep an eye out for sb.為關注某人的出現,這裡引申為等待某人的來臨。

A: I will remember to go to the restaurant and get together with you tonight.

B: Ok, I'll keep an eye out for you.

> **A**：今晚我會記得去餐廳跟你聚一聚。
> **B**：好的，我會等待你的來臨。

▶▶ main course 主菜

A: I want to order a salad and a soup.

B: How about the main course?

> **A**：我要點一份沙拉和一份湯。
> **B**：那麼主菜吃什麼呢？

▶▶ make a reservation 預訂

A: I want to make a reservation for tonight.

B: How many are you?

A：我想要預訂今晚的座位。

B：你們是幾位呢？

▶▶ on the house 免費

解說

指主人招待。

A：Today is my birthday. Drinks are on the house.

B：Happy birthday.

A：今天是我生日，飲料免費。

B：祝你生日快樂。

▶▶ serve up 上菜

A：It's time to serve up the starter.

B：I'll take care of it right now.

A：該上開胃菜了。

B：我會立刻上菜。

1

▶▶ **try out** 試吃

A : There is a new restaurant opening across from my apartment.

B : Let's try out that new place.

A : 我的公寓對面有一家新開的餐廳。

B : 讓我們去那家新餐廳試吃看看。

(二) 飲食評價與付帳小主題

▶▶ **cup of tea** 喜愛的人或事物

A : Japanese food is my cup of tea. Can you rec-ommend a good restaurant to me?

B : I think you should go to the Harbar Restaurant.

A : 我最喜歡吃日本菜了，你能推薦好的餐廳給我嗎？

B : 我想你應該去哈巴餐廳。

▶▶ heavily seasoned 味道重

A : Would you like some stinky tofu?

B : No, thanks. It's heavily seasoned and not to my taste.

A : 你要吃點臭豆腐嗎？

B : 不，謝謝，它味道重且不合我的口味。

▶▶ light meal 清淡的食物

指吃得少而清淡的一頓飯，有時候中文翻譯為「便餐」。

A : It's time for lunch. I want to have a light meal.

B : I know a good place where we can eat.

A : 吃午餐時間到了，我想吃點清淡的食物。

B : 我知道有一間好餐廳，我們可以去那裡吃。

PART

▶▶ hit the spot 很好吃

指東西好吃或好喝。

A : That dinner really hit the spot. We need to go out for steak more often.

B : We could if it isn't so expensive.

A : 那晚餐真的很好吃，我們真該更常外出吃牛排。

B : 如果它不會很貴，我們可以這麼做。

▶▶ to my liking 好吃

A : I'm a vegetarian. So, I'm off meat.

B : What a shame. The restaurant's steak is to my liking.

A : 我吃素，所以我不吃肉。

B : 真可惜，這間餐廳的牛排很好吃。

▶▶ **out of this world** 超棒／絕無僅有

A : The apple pie is out of this world.

B : Right. I think Susan made it.

A : 蘋果派超棒的。

B : 沒錯，我想那是蘇珊做的。

▶▶ **come to** 總共

A : May I have the check, please?

B : With the tip, that comes to 12 dollars.

A : 可以給我帳單嗎？

B : 加上小費，總共12美元。

▶▶ **go Dutch** 各付各的

A : I buy you dinner.

B : No, let's go Dutch.

A：我請你吃晚餐。

B：不，讓我們各付各的。

▶▶ it's on sb. 請客

A：It's on me.

B：Then I'll treat you next time.

A：我請客。

B：那麼下次我請你。

▶▶ keep the change 零錢不用找

A：That comes to 45 dollars.

B：Here's 50 dollars. Keep the change.

A：總共45美元。

B：這裡是50美元，零錢不用找。

▶▶ share the expense 各自付帳

A: Today is my birthday. I treat you.

B: I think we had better share the expense.

A: 今天是我生日，我請客。

B: 我想我們最好各自付帳。

▶▶ to treat sb. 請客

A: You don't have to pay the bill today. I'll treat you.

B: Thank you. It's on me next time.

A: 今天你不需要付帳，我請客。

B: 謝謝，下次我請你。

05 金錢場景

(一) 有錢小主題

▶▶ **an arm and a leg** 許多錢

指買任何東西要你付出一隻手臂和一隻腳,表示東西很貴,要花很多錢。

A: Check out the new shoes I just bought.

B: Nice. They must have cost you an arm and a leg.

A: 看一下我剛買的新鞋子。

B: 很漂亮,它們一定花掉你很多錢。

▶▶ **be loaded** 很有錢

A: I know you are loaded. Why don't you pay for our dinner?

B: I feel like you need to pay for your own dinner.

A：我知道你很有錢，你為什麼不請我們吃晚餐呢？

B：我覺得你得支付你自己的晚餐。

▶▶ be made of money 很有錢

解說

是錢做成的，表示錢很多。

A：Do you want to buy an iPhone cellphone? The price is about 200 dollars.

B：Do you think I'm made of money?

A：你想要買iPhone手機嗎？價錢大約是200美元。

B：你認為我很有錢嗎？

▶▶ come into a fortune 繼承一筆遺產

A：Wow, new car, new house. Have you come into a fortune?

B：No, I haven't. But I won the state lottery.

PART

A：哇，新車，新房子，你繼承了一筆遺產嗎？

B：不，我沒有，但是我中了州彩券。

▶▶ deep pockets 經濟狀況良好

(解)(說)

直譯為「深口袋」，引申很有錢，經濟狀況良好。

A：The light blue jacket is expensive.

B：Don't worry. Helen has deep pockets.

A：這件淺藍色夾克很貴。

B：不要擔心，海倫經濟狀況良好。

▶▶ have money to burn 非常有錢

(解)(說)

燒錢，表示錢多的用不完。

A：The sapphire bracelet is 300 bucks.

B : Well, I don't have money to burn. I can't afford it.

A : 這藍寶石手鐲是300美元。

B : 嗯，我沒有閒錢，我買不起。

▶▶ pretty penny 很多錢

A : Everyone in show business makes a pretty penny.

B : I know, and they don't even have to work that hard.

A : 在演藝圈，每個人都賺很多錢。

B : 我知道，他們甚至不必那麼辛苦工作。

(二) 沒錢小主題

▶▶ be flat broke 很窮

指半毛錢也沒有。

A : Everyone is flat broke at the end of the month.

B : Me, too. Now I have to manage with 20 dollars until payday.

A : 在月底，每個人都很窮。

B : 我也是一樣，現在我得用20美元支撐到發薪日。

▶▶ be hard up 缺錢

A : Why did you give that guy 10 dollars?

B : He told me a real story about why he is hard up for cash.

A : 你為什麼給那傢伙10美元呢？

B : 他告訴我一個真實故事，來說明他為什麼缺錢。

▶▶ in debt 負債

A : I'm in debt after I spent so much money buying the car.

B : Yes, but at least you look like a rich man.

A : 在我花了那麼多錢買這輛車後，我就負債了。
B : 沒錯，但是至少你看起來像個有錢人。

▶▶ in the hole 負債

A : Going to a university has put me in the hole because the tuition is expensive.

B : But it is worth going to university. You can make more money after graduation from university.

A : 因為學費很貴，上大學讓我負債。
B : 但是上大學是值得的，大學畢業後，你可以賺更多的錢。

▶▶ live beyond sb.'s means 超支

解說
指過著超出自己收入的生活。

A : I don't believe I live beyond my means.

B : You had better save some money for a rainy day.

A : 我不敢相信我生活超支。

B : 你最好存一些錢以防不時之需。

▶▶ make ends meet 收支平衡

A : The new car cost me a lot of money. Now I have to watch every penny to reduce expenses.

B : No wonder you couldn't make ends meet last month.

A : 這輛新車花掉我很多錢，現在我必須精打細算來減少開支。

B : 怪不得你上個月無法讓收支平衡。

▶▶ pinch and scrape 省吃儉用

A : The tuition will be increased next year. I can hardly afford it.

B : So, you have to pinch and scrape to save some money for the tuition.

A : 學費明年會上漲，我快負擔不起了。

B : 所以你要省吃儉用，存一些錢來支付學費。

補充

pinch and scrape = scrape and screw

▶▶ pinch pennies 精打細算

A : Now the prices are increasing. I have to pinch pennies to make ends meet.

B : Luckily, I got a good paying job last month.

A : 物價持續上漲，我必須精打細算來讓收支平衡。

B : 很幸運，上個月我得到一份高薪的工作。

▶▶ tight budget 手頭很緊

A : I have a tight budget. Do you think you can loan me some money?

B : Well, how much do you need?

A : 我手頭很緊，你想你能借給我一些錢嗎？

B : 嗯，你需要多少錢呢？

PART

2

第 **2** 單元

校園學習業餘片語

01 情緒場景

▶▶ **feel like a million dollars** 心情好

A : I feel like a million dollars. My teacher liked the paper I wrote.

B : Maybe we should go out and celebrate.

A : 我心情超好,我的老師喜歡我寫的報告。

B : 或許我們應該出去慶祝一下。

▶▶ **be pissed at sb.** 生氣

A : I am really pissed at myself for not applying for the Academic Senate Scholarship.

B : There are still plenty of other scholarships that you can apply for.

A : 我對自己很生氣,因為沒有申請到學術會議獎學金。

B : 還是有許多別的獎學金,你可以申請。

▶▶ broken hearted 很難過

直譯為「心碎」，引申為很悲傷或沮喪。

A : What would happen if you aren't accepted to Stanford?

B : I will be broken hearted, and pray that U.C. Berkeley accepts me.

A : 你如果沒被史丹佛大學錄取，會怎麼樣呢？

B : 我會很難過，並祈禱加州伯克萊大學會錄取我。

▶▶ cheer sb. up 使某人高興起來

A : Kevin is still depressed about Jennifer's dumping him.

B : Let's take him out tonight and cheer him up.

A : 凱文因珍妮佛甩了他，心情仍在沮喪中。

B : 我們今晚帶他出去，讓他高興起來。

▶▶ chill out 放鬆一下

解說
指在緊張或辛苦工作後，來放鬆身心。

 : What are you thinking about doing this week-end?

B : I think I am just going to stay home and chill out.

A : 你這週末想做什麼呢？

B : 我想我只打算留在家裡放鬆一下。

補充
chill out = take it easy

▶▶ down in the dumps 心情不好

解說
dumps 情緒低落。

 : You seem very down in the dumps. What's wrong?

B : I feel so down about failing my driving test.

A : 你似乎心情很不好，出了什麼事？
B : 我駕駛考試不及格，心情很不好。

▶▶ lose sb.'s temper 發脾氣

A : If you lose your temper in the morning, you will be in a bad mood all day.

B : You're right. I'll try to relax and chill out.

A : 如果你在早上發脾氣，你整天都會心情不好。
B : 你說得很對，我會盡量放輕鬆和冷靜下來。

lose sb.'s temper = lose sb.'s cool

▶▶ raise the roof 掀翻屋頂／大聲喧鬧

A : We are really going to raise the roof at the party tonight.

B : Yeah? It's going to be a lot of fun.

A：我們今晚將在派對上大聲喧鬧。

B：是嗎？那將非常有趣。

▶▶ **get sour** 心情不好

get sour 直譯為「變酸」，用在形容東西，則指東西壞了，如 The milk got sour.（牛奶壞了）；若用在形容人，則指人的心情變得不好。

A：Every time we lose, the coach always gets sour.

B：Well, if he had us practice more, maybe we wouldn't have lost so much.

A：每次我們輸了，教練總是心情不好。

B：嗯，如果他有讓我們再多練習點，可能我們就不會輸那麼多。

▶▶ **get under sb.'s skin** 惹怒某人

 解說
使某人不舒服。

A : The noise coming from my neighbor's house is beginning to get under my skin.

B : Maybe we should go over there and tell them to keep it down.

A : 來自鄰居家的噪音開始惹怒我。

B : 或許我們應該過去那裡，告訴他們小聲一點。

▶▶ **give sb. a heart attack** 吃驚害怕

 解說
某物使人吃驚恐懼。

A : Why did you jump out of the bushes like that? You could have given somebody a heart attack.

B : Sorry. It's Halloween, and the time of year to scare people.

PART

A 你為什麼那樣從矮樹叢裡跳出來呢？你可能會讓某人吃驚害怕。

B 抱歉，今天是萬聖節，而每年的這個時候就是要嚇人。

▶▶ in a good mood 心情好

A I failed to pass the midterm. Now I am not in a good mood.

B Let's go out and see a movie today. That will make you feel better.

A 我期中考不及格，現在我心情不好。

B 讓我們今天出去看電影，那會讓你感覺好一些。

▶▶ on cloud nine 十分高興

指高興得像飛到九霄雲外。

A I am on cloud nine. I scored high in the exam.

B: Great. I am so proud of you.

A: 我十分高興，我考試得了高分。

B: 太棒了，我為你感到驕傲。

▶▶ on top of the world 十分高興

到達世界的頂端，就會很得意，欣喜若狂。

A: David is on top of the world after getting a research grant.

B: He has been doing so well. Everyone knows that he is very clever and intelligent.

A: 大衛在得到研究補助後，整個人欣喜若狂。

B: 他一直表現出色，每個人都知道他聰明透頂。

▶▶ out of sorts 不高興

來自以前印刷時，排字工人發覺鉛字（sort）不齊全，就會不高興。

A: I have been depressed lately and cannot stop eating.

B: I also can't stop eating when I feel out of sorts.

A: 我最近情緒低落，而且一直不停的吃。

B: 當我覺得不高興時，我也會不停的吃。

▶▶ out of spirits 沒精神

A: You have been out of spirits lately. What is the matter?

B: I got a low grade on my last lab report.

A: 你最近一直沒精神，發生什麼事了？

B: 我上次實驗報告拿到低分。

▶▶ have a grand time 玩得很愉快

此片語中的 grand，可用 good、great、wonderful 來替代。

A : What was the trip to Alaska like?

B : We had a grand time, looking at the beautiful scenery, and hiking alongside a glacier.

A : 阿拉斯加旅行怎麼樣呢？

B : 我玩得很愉快，看美麗的景色，和沿著冰河邊徒步旅行。

▶▶ upset sb. 讓某人很生氣

A : The fact that you forgot our anniversary really upset me.

B : I am so sorry, honey. What can I do to make it up to you?

A : 你忘記我們週年紀念日，讓我很生氣。

B : 親愛的，對不起，我能做些什麼來補償你呢？

02 比賽場景

▶▶ **an ugly display** 差勁表現

 解說

指行為惡劣，做了或說了不應該的事情。

A: The Giants pitcher put on a real ugly display last night.

B: I know. He gave up over 10 runs in just 3 innings.

A: 昨晚這巨人隊投手表現得很差勁。

B: 我知道，他在短短的3局內失掉超過10分。

▶▶ **be really something** 真的很了不起

 解說

誇獎人的片語，只用於男性，而此片語主詞必須是人。

A: Barry Bonds is really something. He hit 73 home runs last year.

B: Well, he might not have hit so many homeruns if he wasn't on steroids.

：貝瑞邦茲真的很了不起，他去年擊出了73支全壘打。

B'：嗯，如果他沒有服類固醇，他就不能擊出那麼多支全壘打。

補充

might have + 過去分詞，表示對過去發生的事情進行推測。

▶▶ **be tied** 平手

： Did you watch the rest of the baseball game last night?

B'： No, they were tied until at least till the 15th inning, and then I fell asleep.

A'：你昨晚有觀看餘下的棒球比賽嗎？

B'：沒有，它們至少到15局為止是平手，接著我就睡著了。

補充

fall asleep 睡著了。

▶▶ give it sb.'s all 盡力而為

A : Coach, I am really nervous about pitching to-day's game.

B : All I expect from you is to give it your all. Now, go get them.

> **A :** 教練，今天的比賽上場投球，讓我很緊張。
>
> **B :** 我盼望的是你盡力而為，現在，上場吧。

▶▶ give sb. a shot 給某人機會

A : Do you think the coach will let you play start-ing pitcher?

B : I asked him to give me a shot, and he said, "we'll see."

> **A :** 你想教練會讓你當先發投手嗎？
>
> **B :** 我要求他給我機會，而他說：「我們會看看。」

▶▶ lose sb.'s edge 某人失去優勢

A : I used to be better than Scott at golf, but now he's winning.

B : You must be losing your edge. Maybe you should practice more.

A : 我過去高爾夫球打得比史考特好，但現在是他贏球。

B : 你一定失去了優勢，或許你應該多加練習。

keep sb.'s edge = stay sharp 保持優勢。

▶▶ knock out 擊倒

A : How was the title fight last night?

B : You should have been there. Mike Tyson was knocked out cold.

A : 昨晚的冠軍拳擊賽如何呢？

B : 你應該到現場，邁克泰森被擊倒在地不醒人事。

補充

cold 失去知覺。

▶▶ mark my words 聽我說

 Mark my words; we do not stand a chance against the Stanford basketball team.

B: You need to stop being so pessimistic, and have some hope.

A: 聽我說;我們沒有機會打敗史丹佛籃球隊。

B: 你得停止悲觀,抱持希望。

▶▶ on a roll 正走運

解說

指運氣好,做事越來越順,且不斷地有佳績出現。

 Our team is on a roll. We are on an eight-game winning streak.

B: Hopefully, you'll break the old record of 10 straight wins.

：我們隊正在走運，我們8連勝。

 ：希望，你們會打破10連勝的記錄。

補充

winning streak 連勝。

▶▶ **out of control 失控**

解說

失去控制，而陷入模糊與混亂的感覺。

A：Soccer fans are rowdier than all other sports fans.

B：Maybe that's true in other parts of the world, but in America, football fans are the most out of control.

A：足球迷比其他運動球迷更為粗暴。

B：或許在某些國家真的是這樣，但是在美國，足球迷是最為失控的。

補 充

out of control = out of hand

 play sb.'s part 扮演好自己的角色

解 說

強調各盡其責。

A: If everyone plays his part in tomorrow's game, the other team won't stand a chance.

B: Under your coaching. Let's kick their butts.

A: 如果在明天的比賽中每個人扮演好自己的角色，對方球隊將不會有機會的。

B: 我們全聽教練的，讓我們打敗他們。

 ride on sth. 依靠某事

A: Why did you bet so much money on the Super Bowl?

B: I'm riding on the odds in the newspaper. This should be a for sure bet.

> **A** : 你為什麼在超級盃上，下注那麼多錢呢？
>
> **B** : 我依據報紙上的機率，這應該是穩贏的賭注。

▶▶ rub sb.'s nose in 揭某人的底

直譯為「擦某人鼻子」，引申為「揭某人的底」，而引起他人的注意。

> **A** : No matter how many times you play ping pong with me, I always win.
>
> **B** : Why do you always have to rub my nose in it?

> **A** : 無論你跟我打乒乓球多少次，我總是贏。
>
> **B** : 你為什麼老是要揭我的底呢？

▶▶ rough stuff 犯規

指暴力行為，但在比賽時，指「犯規」。

A : The hockey referees told the players of both teams, "no rough stuff or the game will be canceled."

B : It doesn't sound like the game is going to be too exciting then.

A : 這曲棍球裁判告訴雙方球員：「不准犯規，否則比賽將被取消。」

B : 那麼聽起來好像比賽不會太刺激。

▶▶ **save the day** 扭轉敗局

A : Today's game ball goes to Scott. He saved the day with a home run in the 9th inning.

B : Only 2 more wins to go, and we're in the play-offs!

A : 史考特打出今天決勝負的一球，他在9局以全壘打來扭轉敗局。

B : 只要再贏2場，我們就會進入季後賽！

補充
game ball 決勝負的一球，最後一球。

▶▶ **That's the spirit.** 這樣就對啦

 Okay, fine, I'll give it a shot.

 That's the spirit. I know you'll kick some butt in the singing competition.

 很好，我會試一試。

 這樣就對啦，我知道你會在歌唱比賽中大勝。

 補充
kick some butt 獲得成功。

▶▶ **the last laugh** 最後勝利

 解說
直譯為「最後的笑」，指某人做某事，大家都說他不會成功，但是最後他成功了。

 We were winning the game until the last in-ning.

B : It looks like the other team had the last laugh thanks to that home run in the 9th inning.

A : 在最後一局前，我們都是比賽領先。

B : 聽起來好像由於第9局的全壘打，另一支球隊獲得了最後勝利。

▶▶ tough break 不幸

A : Our best player has sprained his ankle and cannot play in today's game.

B : What a tough break. Now we don't stand a chance.

A : 我們最棒的球員扭傷了腳踝，不能參加今天的比賽。

B : 多麼不幸啊，我們現在沒有機會獲勝了。

▶▶ try out for 參加選拔

A : I am thinking about trying out for the football team at school.

B : Are you sure you can handle school, work, and the school team?

A : 我正在考慮參加學校的足球隊選拔。

B : 你確定你能應付課業、工作和球隊嗎？

handle sth. 應付，處理。

▶▶ turn over a new leaf
重新開始 / 開始新生活

A : The doctor said if I don't quit smoking and drinking, the chances of getting cancer and liver disease are very high.

B : It sounds like you need to turn over a new leaf, and quit those bad habits.

A : 醫生說如果我不戒菸酒，得到癌症和肝病的機會會很高。

B : 聽起來好像你需要展開新生活，停止那些有害的習慣。

▶▶ up against 對抗

用在比賽或戰爭中，面對你的對手比你強大時使用。

A: Today we go up against the 1st place team. I expect everyone to give it their all.

B: Don't worry, coach. Today's win will be for you.

A: 今天我們要對抗第一名的隊伍，我期待每個人全力以赴。

B: 不要擔心，教練；今天的勝利是屬於你的。

▶▶ up to speed 瞭解情況

指對某件事瞭若指掌。

A: Are you sure you're prepared for the Final?

B: I missed the last 3 classes because I was out of town, but Jerry has brought me up to speed.

PART

A：你確定做好期末考準備了嗎？

B：因為我不在城裡，而錯過最後3節課，但是傑瑞已經讓我瞭解狀況。

▶▶ until the fat lady sings 沒有結束之前

直譯為「直到肥女人唱歌之前」，延伸為最後關鍵結束後，勝負才會自然分曉。

A：We're down by 2 runs, and it's already the ninth inning. We don't stand a chance.

B：Hey, it's not over until the fat lady sings.

A：我們落後2分，而都已經是第9局，我們沒有機會了。

B：嗨，比賽沒有結束之前，一切都還不一定。

127

PART

▶▶ **wear down** 使疲勞

 解說

指讓某人精疲力竭。

A: If you wait any longer, you're going to lose the boxing match.

B: I'm just wearing him down. Don't worry; I'm just about to make my move.

A: 如果你再等下去，就會輸掉這場拳賽。

B: 我只是消耗他體力，不要擔心；我正要採取行動。

 補充

make sb.'s move 採取行動。

03 購物場景

▶▶ **a good buy** 很便宜

A'：The overcoat cost me 20 dollars. It's kind of pricy.

B'：But I think it's really a good buy.

A'：大衣花掉我20美元，它有點貴。
B'：但是我認為它真的很便宜。

▶▶ **buy one get one free** 買一送一

A'：I heard only today there is buy one get one free at Starbucks.

B'：It's time to treat you.

A'：我聽說星巴克只有今天買一送一。
B'：正好我可以請你。

▶▶ clearance sale 清倉大拍賣

指商店銷售以減少存貨。

A : I heard the boutique is having a clearance sale.

B : Great. I don't want to miss such a good chance.

A : 我聽說這家精品店正在清倉大拍賣。

B : 太棒了,我不想錯過如此的好機會。

▶▶ early bird ticket 早鳥票

A : I want to buy cheap airline tickets to London seven months later.

B : Maybe you should book early bird tickets on-line in advance.

A : 我想要買七個月後去倫敦的便宜機票。

B : 或許你應該在網路上預先訂購早鳥票。

▶▶ for a song 很便宜地

解說
指廉價買到東西。

A : The clothes look gorgeous. They must cost you a lot of money.

B : Actually, I bought them for a song at a garage sale.

A : 衣服看起來很漂亮,它們一定花費你很多錢。

B : 事實上,我在車庫拍賣中很便宜地買到它們。

▶▶ for sale 出售

A : I heard the apartment is for sale.

B : But I heard it is for rent.

A : 我聽說這公寓要出售。

B : 但是我聽說它是要出租。

▶▶ highway robbery 敲竹槓

直譯爲「攔路搶劫」，引申爲「敲竹槓」。

A : This dress is beautiful. The price is 1,000 dollars.

B : That's simply highway robbery. I think it is not worth that much.

A : 這件裙子很漂亮，要價1,000美元。

B : 那簡直是敲竹槓，我覺得不值那麼多錢。

▶▶ knock off 減價

A : If you take both pairs of sandals, I'll knock 10 dollars off.

B : I'll take them.

A : 如果你買兩雙涼鞋，可以便宜10美元。

B : 我買了。

▶▶ look around 逛逛

A : Today is Christmas Day. I want to look around the mall.

B : Don't be silly. The mall is not open today, as it's Christmas Day.

A : 今天是聖誕節,我想要去逛逛購物中心。

B : 別傻了,因為是聖誕節,購物中心今天沒有開。

look around = browse around

▶▶ pay off 付清

A : In three months, I can finally afford to pay off my car.

B : Then, can we go on a vacation?

A : 在三個月後,我終於可以付清我的車款。

B : 那麼,我們可以去度假了嗎?

▶▶ sell off 廉價銷售

因爲需要錢，而便宜賣出。

A: These old furniture are sold off at half price.

B: I think now it is a great time to get bargains.

A: 這些老舊家具都是以半價銷售。

B: 我想現在是買便宜貨的好時機。

▶▶ sell out 賣光

A: I've been trying to score tickets to Harry Potter all week.

B: I told you they were probably going to be sold out.

A: 我整個星期都試著想得到哈利波特的票。

B: 我告訴你，它們很可能早就賣光了。

補充

score 成功地獲得。

▶▶ **trade in 舊換新**

A : I bought an iPhone last month but a new one is coming out soon.

B : Sounds like it is time to trade it in for a new one.

A : 我上月買一台iPhone，但是新款很快就出來。

B : 聽起來好像是舊換新的時候到了。

▶▶ **rip-off 敲竹槓**

解說

指漫天要價，價錢不合理，就是要坑騙客人。

A : I want to buy the new suit but it is too expensive.

B : Don't buy it and I feel it is a rip-off.

A：我想買這套衣服，但是它太貴了。

B：不要買它，而我覺得它是敲竹槓。

▶▶ **window shopping** 逛櫥窗

指逛商店，只看而不買。

A：I don't have money to buy things.

B：It's OK. We can go window shopping.

A：我沒有錢買東西。

B：沒關係，我們可以逛櫥窗而不花錢。

04 交通場景

▶▶ be caught in 遇到

A: It looks as if Jeff is not going to practice on time again.

B: I bet he's just caught in traffic.

> **A**: 看起來好像傑夫不再準時練習。
> **B**: 我打賭他剛好是遇到交通阻塞。

▶▶ car trouble 車子故障

A: It' about time you came. We were about to start the movie without you.

B: Sorry, I had some car trouble on the way over there.

> **A**: 該是你到達的時候，我們不等你，要準備開始放電影了。
> **B**: 對不起，我在來的途中，車子故障了。

▶▶ floor it 開到最快

指把油門踩到最大，開到最快。

A : I will be late for school. If you floor it, we might make it in time.

B : I'd rather be late than get another speeding ticket.

A : 我上學將會遲到，如果你開到最快，我們可能會及時到達。

B : 我寧願遲到，也不願拿到另一張的超速罰單。

▶▶ get away with 逃脫懲罰

指做壞事，而未受懲罰。

A : Scott was pulled over by the police and talked him out of another ticket.

B : That guy gets away with everything.

：史考特開車時被警察攔下來，而且說服警察不要再開罰單。

B：那傢伙每次都能逃脫懲罰。

補充

talk sb. out of sth. 說服某人不要做某事。

▶▶ get creamed 遭重創

A：On my way to work today, I saw someone on a motorcycle get creamed by a truck.

B：Ouch! Do you think he survived?

A：今天去工作的途中，我看見騎摩托車的人被卡車重創。

B：哎喲，你想他還活著嗎？

▶▶ get nailed 重罰

指陷入大麻煩中，而遭受處罰。

A : If you continue to drink and drive, you're liable to get nailed by the police.

B : You're probably right, but the taxis are too expensive.

A : 如果你繼續喝酒開車，很容易就會被警察重罰。

B : 你或許說得是對的，但是坐計程車太貴了。

▶▶ **give sb. a lift** 給某人搭便車

A : Can you give me a lift to work tomorrow?

B : Sure. Is your car acting up again?

A : 你明天能讓我搭便車去工作嗎？

B : 當然可以，你的車子又發生故障了嗎？

give sb. a lift = give sb. a ride

▶▶ pull over 命令停在路邊

指開車行駛到路邊停下來。

A: When the police pulled me over, they told me to have a seat in the back of the patrol car. I thought for sure I was going to jail.

B: Why would they take you to jail for speeding?

A: 當警察命令我把車停在路邊時，他們告訴我要坐到巡邏車的後座，我想我肯定會被關進監獄裡。

B: 他們為什麼會因超速而把你送進監獄裡呢？

have a seat = take a seat 請坐。

▶▶ run a red light 闖紅燈

A: What happened to your car?

B: Someone ran a red light, and their car nailed me from the side.

PART

A：你的車發生什麼事呢？

B：有人闖紅燈，他們的車從旁邊撞到我。

▶▶ stay clear of 避開

A：Make sure to stay clear of the highway. There was a big accident, and traffic is backed up for miles.

B：Thanks for the advice. I'll take the expressway home.

A：你一定要避開公路，有一個大的意外事件，交通阻塞了好幾英里。

B：謝謝你的建議，我會上高速公路回家。

▶▶ stay cool 鎮靜

A：Oh, no. We're being pulled over by the cops.

B：Just stay cool, and let me do the talking.

142

A: 哦，真糟糕，我們被警察攔下來了。

B: 鎮靜些，讓我來跟警察解釋。

do the talking 負責說話。

▶▶ step on it 加快速度

A: I'm running late for my flight. Step on it, please.

B: It'll cost you an extra $20 if you want me to speed.

A: 我快趕不上我的班機了，請加快速度。

B: 如果你要我超速，得要另外再付20美元。

PART

05 愛情場景

▶▶ a second chance 第二次機會

A: Amanda, what can I do for you to give me a second chance?

B: I'm sorry, Brian. I just don't have feelings for you anymore.

A: 艾曼達,我該怎麼做,你才能給我第二次機會呢?

B: 對不起,布萊恩,我只是不再對你有感覺了。

▶▶ be expecting a child 懷孕

A: I danced with joy when I found out Rebecca was expecting a child.

B: That must have been a really special moment.

A: 當我知道麗蓓卡懷孕時,我高興地跳起舞來。

B: 那一定是一個很特殊的時刻。

dance with joy 高興地跳舞。

▶▶ break off 解除

A : Dennis and Jill broke off their engagement.

B : I heard that Jill caught Dennis cheating on her.

> **A** : 丹尼斯和吉兒解除婚約了。
> **B** : 我聽說吉兒逮到丹尼斯對她不忠。

cheat on 對…不忠。

▶▶ break up 分手

A : Why did you and Jane break up?

B : She caught me looking at other girls.

> **A** : 你為什麼跟珍分手呢？
> **B** : 她逮到我看別的女生。

▶▶ have a crush on 暗戀

A：I thought you hated musicals. What made you have a change of heart?

B：I found out Emily was going, and I have a crush on her.

A：我以為你討厭歌舞劇,什麼讓你改變想法呢?

B：我打聽出艾蜜莉會去,而我暗戀她。

find out 發現到,change of heart 改變看法(是指改變態度、觀念或想法)。

▶▶ have a history 有一段感情

解說

直譯為「有歷史」,引申為「有一段感情」或「有一段不愉快的事情」。

A：I never knew you two had previously met.

B：Oh, yeah. Jane and I have a history together. We used to date in college.

A : 我從不知道你們兩人曾經相識。

B : 哦，對啊，珍和我有一段共同的感情，在大學時，我們經常約會。

▶▶ hit on 搭訕

此片語也有「碰上」的意思，如 I care for the girl I hit on at the party last night.我喜歡我昨晚在舞會上遇見的女孩。

A : That guy just hit on me.

B : Did you give him your phone number?

A : 這傢伙剛搭訕我。

B : 你有給他你的電話號碼嗎？

PART

▶▶ like apples and oranges
兩件無法比較的事物

指像蘋果與橘子一樣是沒辦法比較的，強調事情是完全不同，
沒辦法互相比較。

A: I don't know how Fred and Betty have stayed with each other for so long.

B: I know. They are like apples and oranges.

A: 我不知道佛瑞德和貝蒂如何長久相守在一起。

B: 我懂你的意思，他們就像是兩件無法比較的事物。

▶▶ like peas and carrots 形影不離

A: How are you getting along with your girl-friend?

B: We go together like peas and carrots.

A：你和你的女朋友相處如何？

B：我們像豌豆和胡蘿蔔一樣形影不離。

▶▶ make up with sb. 與某人重歸於好

A：Are you and Mary still broken up?

B：Actually, we made up with each other last night.

A：你和瑪麗現在還是分手嗎？

B：事實上，我們昨晚重歸於好了。

▶▶ one night stand 一夜情

one night stand 出自以前旅行戲團在一處只演出一場之意，後來引申到兩個陌生男女的短暫親密接觸，且雙方事後不須互相瞭解與負責。

A：Why didn't you go home with that guy at the bar last night?

B : I had the feeling he was only looking for a one night stand.

A : 昨晚你為什麼在酒吧沒有跟那個傢伙回家呢？

B : 我有一種感覺，他只是在尋找一夜情。

▶▶ **love at first sight** 一見鍾情

A : From the moment I laid eyes on you, I fell in love with you.

B : So, I guess you believe in love at first sight.

A : 從我第一眼看到你，我就愛上你了。

B : 所以，我猜想你相信一見鍾情。

▶▶ **out of sb.'s league** 配不上某人

此片語句型為 A be out of B's league，A 的層級比 B 高出很多，指「B 配不上 A」許多，非 B 所能及。

150

A : I'd love to ask Mary to a dance, but she's out of my league.

B : You'll never know unless you build up the courage to ask her.

A : 我想邀請瑪麗去跳舞，但是我配不上她。

B : 除非你鼓起勇氣去邀請她，否則你永遠不會知道結果。

▶▶ **set sb. up with** 介紹某人認識

用在介紹異性，就是牽線跟某人約會。

A : I am going out with Kim tonight.

B : Do you think you can set me up with one of your friends?

A : 今晚我要和金出去玩。

B : 你認為你能介紹我跟你的某位朋友認識嗎？

set sb. up = fix sb.up = hook sb. up

▶▶ **sweet talk** 甜言蜜語

解說

此片語本身是名詞也是動詞。

: I have a date with Dave this Friday.

: Did his sweet talk work on you again?

: 這星期五我和戴夫有個約會。

: 他的甜言蜜語再次對你產生效用了嗎？

 人際場景

▶▶ **at sb.'s service** 隨時為某人提供服務

指隨時為某人提供幫忙或服務。

A: Would you please give me a hand?

B: Sure. I'm always at your service.

A: 請你幫個忙好嗎？
B: 沒問題，我隨時為你提供服務。

▶▶ **be through with** 結束

此片語常用在男女戀愛關係的結束。

A: I heard you and Stacey are having problems again.

B: I am through with her once and for all. She cheated on me, and broke my drum set.

153

PART

A : 我聽說你和斯特西又出現了問題。

B : 我跟她之間徹底完了,她欺騙我,且打破我的爵士鼓。

once and for all 一次了結地,drum set 爵士鼓。

▶▶ **between you and me**
我們之間的祕密

A : It's between you and me. Please you don't tell anyone.

B : I promise I'll keep the secret.

A : 這是我們之間的祕密,請你不要告訴別人。

B : 我保證我會保守祕密。

▶▶ **call it square** 扯平了

A : I owe you $10 from last week, so I just pay for your movie ticket and we'll call it square.

B : Sounds like a good deal to me.

：上週我欠你10美元，所以我只需付你電影票的錢，然後我們就扯平了。

B：這方法聽起來很不錯。

▶▶ catch up on things 敘敘舊

解說

指好好的聚一下，聊聊天。

A：Why couldn't you show up for dinner tonight?

B：I bumped into Ashley at the mall today. We haven't seen each other in years, so we went out for coffee to catch up on things.

：你為什麼今晚不能來吃晚餐呢？

B：我今天在購物中心遇到艾希莉，我們好多年沒見面了，所以出去喝咖啡敘敘舊。

補充

in years 多年來。

155

▶▶ **built a rapport** 建立和諧的關係

rapport 融洽。

A : The best way to gain customer loyalty is to build a rapport with them.

B : I agree with that. If the customers trusts you, then they will be more than likely to buy things from you again.

A : 獲得顧客忠誠度最好的方法是跟他們建立和諧的關係。

B : 我同意,如果顧客相信你,那麼他們會很願意再向你購買東西。

▶▶ **drop in** 拜訪

指不預約的短時間拜訪,強調突然性,drop in+地點,drop in on+人。

A: After I get settled in my new apartment, feel free to drop in anytime whenever you like.

B: Ok, I will probably come and visit you next week.

A: 我在新公寓安頓好以後，只要你喜歡，隨時都可以來拜訪。

B: 好的，我下週可能會過去拜訪。

drop in = drop at = drop by = drop over

▶▶ **fall out** 鬧翻

A: Why didn't you go to Evan's wedding?

B: We had a bit of a falling out a year ago, and he just didn't invite me.

A: 你為什麼沒有去伊凡的婚禮呢？

B: 一年前，我們有點事鬧翻了，所以他沒邀請我。

▶▶ get on sb.'s nerves 使某人厭煩

A: Andy has been getting on my nerves lately. All he does is brag about his new car.

B: I have just been ignoring him.

A: 安迪最近一直令我厭煩,只會炫耀他的新車。
B: 我最近一直不理睬他。

▶▶ give sb. a hand 幫忙某人

A: Could you give me a hand with the chores?

B: No problem. It's my pleasure.

A: 你能幫我一起做家務嗎?
B: 沒問題,這是我的榮幸。

▶▶ go way back 交情很深

指兩個人認識很長時間。

A : How long have you known Bruce?

B : Bruce and I go way back. We have known each other since kindergarten.

A : 你認識布魯斯多久了？

B : 布魯斯和我交情很深，自從幼稚園開始，我們就互相認識。

▶▶ **had a bad rap** 名聲不好

A : I feel bad for Steven. Nothing seems to ever go his way.

B : Yeah, he's had a bad rap, but I'm sure his luck will turn around.

A : 我替史蒂文難過，他似乎事事都不順。

B : 是啊，他名聲不好，但是我確定他的運氣會好轉。

▶▶ leave out 冷落

A: I invited Mike to go fishing with us, so he wouldn't feel left out.

B: You should have at least discussed it with me first. There are already too many people going.

A: 我邀請麥克跟我們去釣魚，如此一來他將不會覺得被冷落。

B: 你至少應該先跟我討論，目前要去的人已經很多了。

▶▶ mix up 誤會

一般翻譯為誤解，或者是把某人搞糊塗。

A: My mom told me you came over to see me last night.

B: There must be a mix up because I was at the movies with Mary last night.

A：我媽媽告訴我昨晚你來找我。

B：這其中一定有些誤會，因為昨晚我跟瑪麗去看電影。

(補)(充)

mix up = misunderstanding = confusion

▶▶ out of the loop 脫離了圈子

(解)(說)

隱喻為搞不清楚狀況，或對某事不知情。

A：How are things going with all the guys from school?

B：I am not too sure. I've been out of the loop ever since I moved to New York.

A：你和學校裡的人相處得怎麼樣呢？

B：我不太清楚，自從我搬到紐約，我就已經脫離了那個圈子。

▶▶ party animal 喜歡參加宴會的人

解說

英文中常用 animal 來形容有獨特才能或有特殊興趣的人。

: It's hard to believe Jeff is married with two kids already.

: I know. That guy was such a party animal in college. I could never see him getting married, let alone having children.

A: 很難相信傑夫已經結婚，並有兩個小孩。

B: 我知道，那傢伙在大學時是超級喜歡參加聚會的人，我從不曾想過他會結婚，更別說有小孩了。

▶▶ tell a soul 告訴任何人

soul 本來是靈魂、精神的意思，在一些歌詞中出現的 soul 是指
稱人，而這裡的 a soul 等於 anyone。

A : Don't tell a soul. It's a secret.

B : You can trust me. I won't tell anyone.

A : 不要告訴任何人，這是一個祕密。

B : 你可以相信我，我不會告訴任何人。

▶▶ turn down 拒絕

A : Are you OK? You look blue.

B : My application for admission was turned down.

A : 你還好嗎？你看起來心情不好。

B : 我的入學申請被拒絕了。

07 時間場景

▶▶ **at once** 同時

A: I can play the piano and sing a song at once.

B: I think you are a talented musician.

A: 我可以同時彈鋼琴和唱歌。

B: 我想你是一位有才華的音樂家。

▶▶ **a matter of time** 時間問題

A: It's only a matter of time before global warming.

B: I think that time has already come.

A: 全球暖化只是時間的問題。

B: 我想那時間已經來臨了。

常用類似片語有 a matter of money 金錢問題。

PART

▶▶ **any minute** 隨時

時間過很快，隨時會發生。

A: Jerry should be arriving any minute.

B: If he doesn't come within the next 5 minutes, we'll cut the cake without him.

> A: 傑利應該隨時會到達。
>
> B: 如果他在接下來的5分鐘內沒到，我們就不等他，直接切蛋糕了。

▶▶ **at the last minute** 到最後一刻

A: Janice, I didn't know you were coming to the party. What a pleasant surprise.

B: I decided to come at the last minute.

> A: 珍妮絲，我不知道你會來參加宴會，真高興在這兒見到你。
>
> B: 我在最後一刻才決定要來。

165

▶▶ be real short 時間很短

是很快的意思。

A: Can you visit me during your trip to New York?

B: Unfortunately, this trip is going to be real short.

A: 在紐約旅行期間,你能來看我嗎?

B: 很不幸地,這趟旅行時間很短。

▶▶ be running out of time 快沒時間了

A: I still need to make the airline reservation for the Hawaii trip.

B: You'd better hurry. The promotion ends at 6 p.m. tomorrow, and you're running out of time.

A: 我還需要預訂到夏威夷旅行的機票。

B: 你最好快點,這促銷明天晚上6點結束,你快沒時間了。

▶▶ from now on 今後

A : From now on, I'm going to attend all of my classes.

B : What if there's an emergency?

> **A** : 今後，我會去上每一堂課。
>
> **B** : 如果有緊急事件發生怎麼辦呢？

▶▶ hold up a second 稍等一下

A : Are you ready to go? I have the engine running already.

B : Hold up a second, I have to grab my jacket.

> **A** : 你準備好出發了嗎？我已經發動引擎了。
>
> **B** : 稍等一下，我必須拿我的夾克。

PART

▶▶ in time 及時

 : Do you think you can catch the last bus in time?

 : I think I can make it.

> : 你想你可以及時趕上最後一班公車嗎？
> : 我想我可以趕上。

▶▶ moment of truth 關鍵時刻

解說
指有決定性的時刻。

 : Now is the moment of truth. Are you ready to see whether you've been accepted to Stanford or not?

 : Just open the damn envelope. I can't wait anymore.

> : 現在是關鍵時刻，你準備好看看你是否已經被史丹佛大學錄取嗎？
> : 打開該死的信封，我無法再等了。

▶▶ **no time at all** 沒花多少時間

A : How long did it take you to finish your exam?

B : Actually, it took me no time at all. I finished in 15 minutes.

> A : 你花了多少時間才完成考試呢？
> B : 事實上，沒花我多少時間，我在15分鐘內考完。

▶▶ **on the spot** 當場

指強調立即性。

A : How come you didn't have to work today?

B : My boss said I was being rude to a customer, and fired me on the spot.

> A : 你今天為什麼不必上班呢？
> B : 我老闆說我對一位客人很粗魯，而當場解雇我。

▶▶ on time 準時

A：I can't hand in the paper on time.

B：You should tell your teacher and ask for an extension on your paper.

A：我不能準時交報告。

B：你應該告訴你的老師，請求延期繳交你的報告。

▶▶ some other day 改天

A：Would you like to accompany me to the mall?

B：Maybe some other day. I am busy right now.

A：你想不想陪我去購物中心？

B：或許改天吧，我現在很忙。

PART 2

▶▶ take a rain check 改天

A： Would you like to have dinner with me tonight?

B： Can I take a rain check? I already have plans with my son to see a movie.

> **A：** 今晚你想要跟我一起去吃晚餐嗎？
> **B：** 我能改天嗎？我跟我兒子已經計畫去看電影。

▶▶ there isn't a moment to lose
沒有時間了

 解說
指沒有時間可以耽擱延誤。

A： Our flight leaves in one hour.

B： There isn't a moment to lose. Let's get going.

> **A：** 我們班機在1小時後起飛。
> **B：** 沒有時間了，我們出發吧。

▶▶ **think ahead** 提早

指提前打算，同時要想得長遠。

A : I want to pass the exam with flying colors.

B : Then you had better think ahead and prepare for it.

> **A** : 我想要高分通過考試。
>
> **B** : 那麼你最好提早準備。

▶▶ **wait a minute** 等一下

A : I'll race you to the bus stop.

B : Wait a minute. Let me tie my shoe first.

> **A** : 我和你比賽看誰先到公車站。
>
> **B** : 等一下，讓我先綁鞋帶。

▶▶ **wait for** 等待

 : We've been waiting for you in the car for 15 minutes. What's the holdup?

 : I'll be out in 5 minutes. Let me just finished getting dressed.

 : 我們已經在車裡面等你15分鐘了，什麼事耽誤了呢？

 : 我會在5分鐘內出去，讓我穿完衣服吧。

▶▶ **while we're still young** 快點

解說
用在表示內心有點心急時。

 : Will you just say what's on your mind, while we're still young?

 : Fine, Jenny. Will you marry me?

 : 快點，你想要說什麼？

 : 好吧，珍妮，嫁給我好嗎？

08 加強語氣場景

▶▶ **a deal is a deal.** 說話算話

解說
交易就是交易，就是照合約辦事，來達成交易，強調要遵守信用。

A: You told me if I washed your car you'd give me $10, and a deal is a deal.

B: I will give you the money but you just have to wait until I get paid.

A: 你告訴我，如果我幫你洗車子，你會給我10美元，說話要算話。

B: 我會給你錢，但是你必須等我拿到工資。

▶▶ **all in all** 總而言之

A: What do you think about the University's baseball team?

B: All in all, I think they have a pretty good chance of making the playoffs.

A：你認為大學的棒球隊怎麼樣呢？

B：總而言之，我認為他們很有機會打進季後賽。

▶▶ as a matter of fact 事實上

A：Did you hear Robert died in a car accident last week?

B：As a matter of fact, I was told that he was seriously injured, but not dead.

A：你有聽說羅伯特上週死在車禍中嗎？

B：事實上，我聽說他沒死，只是受傷嚴重。

as a matter of fact = in fact

▶▶ for anything 無論如何

A：I am being sent to the war in the Middle East next week.

B：I wouldn't go there for anything.

A : 下週我會被派到中東打仗。

B : 我無論如何都不會去那裡。

▶▶ for the life of me 怎麼也

專用於否定句,而變成 can't for the life of me,如 I can't for the life of me 可翻譯為「我怎麼也不會去」,簡單的說,就是「我不去」的意思。

A : Would you be interested in going bowling after work on Friday?

B : I wouldn't for the life of me. I think I have something planned.

A : 在星期五下班後,你有興趣打保齡球嗎?

B : 我怎麼也不會去,我想到我有別的計畫。

▶▶ for the world 無論如何

A : Thank you very much for showing up to my graduation.

B : I wouldn't miss it for the world.

A : 非常謝謝你來參加我的畢業典禮。

B : 我無論如何也都不會錯過的。

▶▶ how in the world 到底是怎麼

為 how 的強調語氣。

A : I have been looking all over the place for my wallet. How in the world did you find it?

B : I was cleaning the family room, and found it between the couch cushions.

A : 我一直四處找尋我的皮夾,你到底是怎麼找到它呢?

B : 我清掃家庭娛樂室時,發現它在沙發坐墊之間。

▶▶ in any case 無論如何

A: The deadline for the paper is Friday.

B: In any case, we should try to have it finished by Wednesday, so we have time to proofread and make any adjustments that are needed.

A: 報告截止日期是星期五。

B: 無論如何，我們應該設法在星期三前完成，這樣我們才有時間校正和做必要的修改。

▶▶ in any event 無論如何

A: My brother is deathly ill.

B: In any event, I will be there to support you.

A: 我哥哥病得很重。

B: 無論如何，我都會支持你。

▶▶ next to nothing 算不上什麼

強調差不多，幾乎沒有任何的差別。

A : Compared to rent in the US, the rent in Taiwan is next to nothing.

B : Sure, but so is the income.

A : 跟美國的房租相比，臺灣的價格根本算不上什麼。

B : 沒錯，而且收入也是如此。

▶▶ no matter what 不論什麼

A : My parents want too much from me, and no matter what I do, they are never satisfied.

B : I am sure they mean well. They just want you to be the best you can be.

A : 我父母對我要求很高，而不論我做什麼，他們從不滿意。

B : 我相信他們是善意的，他們只是要你做到最好。

PART

▶▶ not for the world 無論如何也不會

for the world 用在否定句，翻譯爲「無論如何」。

A：Would you like to attend our wedding?

B：I wouldn't miss it for the world.

A：你會想來參加我們婚禮嗎？
B：我無論如何也不會錯過。

▶▶ once and for all 徹底地

強調一勞永逸與最後一次，表示以後永遠不會再發生。

A：I am finished with school once and for all.

B：Do you plan on attending graduate school?

A：我徹底地完成學業了。
B：你有打算就讀研究所嗎？

▶▶ one way or another 無論如何

A: Can you come and visit me next week?

B: As for now, I don't have a means of transportation, but I'll figure out how to get there one way or another.

A: 你下週能過來看我嗎？

B: 到目前為止，我還沒有交通工具，但是無論如何我都會弄清楚怎麼到達那裡。

▶▶ rain or shine 無論如何

也可翻譯為「不論晴天或雨天」。

A: Are you going to the baseball game this weekend?

B: I'll be there rain or shine.

A: 你這週末要去看棒球賽嗎？

B: 無論如何，我都會去。

▶▶ in no way 絕不

A: For all our efforts, we didn't succeed.

B: I'm in no way giving up.

A: 儘管我們努力了，但仍未成功。

B: 我是絕不會放棄的。

▶▶ what on earth 到底是什麼

是 what 的強調語氣，在此片語中，on earth 一般翻譯為「究竟」或「到底」的意思，這裡片語中的 on earth = in the world。

A: What on earth are you up to?

B: I am afraid that I cannot disclose that information.

A: 你到底是在幹什麼啊？

B: 恐怕我不能透露那份資料。

▶▶ what is more important 最重要的是

A: What's your impression of the professor?

B: He has a great sense of humor, but what's more important is that he gives us plenty of food for thought.

> **A:** 你對這位教授的印象如何？
>
> **B:** 他很有幽默感，然而最重要的是，他給了我們許多值得思考的事。

▶▶ what's this I hear about 是怎麼回事

A: What's this I hear about you showing up late to class today?

B: Sorry, my car broke down on the way to school.

> **A:** 我聽說你今天上課遲到，是怎麼回事？
>
> **B:** 抱歉，我的車子在路上拋錨了。

▶▶ where in the world 到底在哪裡

是 where 的加強語氣，在這裡的 in the world 直譯為「在世界上」，而在此片語中，一般翻譯成「究竟」或「到底」的意思。

A: Where in the world have you been? We've been waiting for you for over 30 minutes.

B: Sorry, but I had some car trouble on the way over here.

A: 你到底去了哪裡啊？我們已經等你等超過了30分鐘。

B: 抱歉，我來這裡的路上，車子故障了。

▶▶ without a doubt 毫無疑問

A: Nanotechnology is cutting edge.

B: Without a doubt, it'll revolutionize the products of the future.

A：奈米技術是先進的技術。

B：毫無疑問，它會徹底改變未來的產品。

09 健康場景

▶▶ **be allergic to sth.** 對某物過敏

A: During the springtime, my cats begin to shed their fur, and my allergies begin.

B: Maybe you should just shave your cats, so you won't be allergic to them.

A: 在春天期間,我的貓開始脫毛,於是我開始過敏。

B: 或許你應該幫你的貓剃毛,那麼你就不會過敏了。

▶▶ **catch a cold** 感冒

A: How are you doing? Today you don't look like yourself.

B: You ought to stay away from me. I caught a cold.

A: 你還好嗎?今天你看起來不像你自己。

B: 你應該離我遠一點,我感冒了。

▶▶ check-up 體檢

A : I twisted my ankle and sprained my wrist. I wonder if I hurt somewhere else.

B : I'm no doctor. You should just go get a check-up to be safe.

A : 我扭傷了腳踝和手腕，我想知道我是否有傷到什麼地方。

B : 我不是醫生，為了安全起見，你應該去做體檢。

▶▶ come down with 染上（病）

A : I have come down with a cold. Stay away from me.

B : You had better drink a lot of water and have a lot of rest.

A : 我染上了感冒，離我遠一點。

B : 你最好多喝開水與多休息。

▶▶ fall asleep 麻木

口語一般可指手或腳的麻木。

A : My legs have fallen asleep after sitting here for such a long time.

B : A massage would do wonders for you.

A : 坐在這裡這麼久，我的腿已經麻木了。

B : 按摩對你的腳會有神奇的作用。

▶▶ feel like a million dollars
身體覺得好極了

感到精神很好。

A : Come on. Let's race and loser buys dinner.

B : I feel like a million dollars now. You will be the loser.

A : 來吧，跟你賽跑，輸的人請吃晚餐。

B : 我現在身體覺得好極了，你會是一位輸家。

▶▶ get back in shape 恢復健康

A : The doctor says I can soon get back in shape to play soccer again.

B : That's terrific. It's good news.

A : 醫生說我很快可以恢復健康，可再去踢足球。

B : 太好了，那是一個好消息。

▶▶ go down 消腫

A : I hurt my ankle. It's killing me.

B : You can put some ice on it until the swelling goes down.

A : 我傷了腳踝，痛死我了。

B : 你可以放一些冰在腳踝上，直到消腫為止。

▶▶ go down 吞嚥

A : I am having trouble swallowing these pills my doctor gave me for my headaches.

B : I heard that milk helps them go down easier.

A : 醫生開給我治療頭痛的藥，我在吞嚥上有困難。

B : 我聽說牛奶可幫助藥更容易吞嚥。

have trouble (in) 在…有困難。

▶▶ in perfect shape 健康情況良好

A : I am in perfect shape, so I don't need to see a doctor.

B : I think you should visit a doctor at least once a year for your annual checkup.

A : 我健康情況良好，所以我不需要看醫生。

B : 我想你應該至少一年看一次醫生，做年度體檢。

▶▶ make an appointment with sb.

和某人預約見面

A : I'm calling to make an appointment with Doctor Rose.

B : Well, I will put you through to Doctor Rose.

A : 我打電話是想和羅絲醫生約個時間見面。

B : 好的，我將你的電話轉給羅絲醫生。

▶▶ negative effects 負面作用

A : My doctor tells me not to take any pills on an empty stomach.

B : He is right. It can cause nausea and some negative effects.

A : 我的醫生告訴我不要空腹吃藥。

B : 他說得很對，它可能會引起作嘔和一些負面作用。

▶▶ pull through 恢復健康

A: My doctor told me I'll soon pull through if I stay in the hospital.

B: I think you should follow your doctor's advice.

A: 我的醫生告訴我，我住院會很快地恢復健康。

B: 我想你應該聽醫生的建議。

▶▶ run its course 順其自然發展

指按常規正常發展。

A: I have a high fever. The medicine doesn't seem to help.

B: Don't worry. The cold will run its course.

A: 我發高燒，藥似乎沒有作用。

B: 不要擔心，感冒順其自然就會好。

PART

▶▶ second opinion 第二種意見

由另一專家提供不同的看法。

A：The doctor told me that I need to do surgery to remove the tumor.

B：Are you sure? I think you need a second opinion.

A：醫生告訴我，我需要動手術來切除腫瘤。

B：你確定嗎？我想你需要第二種意見。

▶▶ sore throat 喉嚨疼痛

A：I don't know what I've got. I have a sore throat and stuffy nose.

B：I'm sorry to hear that.

A：我不知道我得了什麼病，我喉嚨痛又鼻塞。

B：聽到這消息我很難過。

▶▶ stay off sb.'s feet 在床上休息

解說

不下地走路，指在床上休息。

A：I am black and blue all over. My shoulder is still hurting.

B：I think you need to stay off your feet for several days.

A：我渾身青一塊紫一塊，肩膀也還在疼。

B：我想你需要在床上休息幾天。

▶▶ take a spill 跌倒

A：What happened to your leg?

B：I took a spill at work, and tore my muscle.

A：你的腿發生了什麼事？

B：我在工作中跌倒，把肌肉拉傷了。

take some medicine 吃點藥

A : I feel drowsy after taking some medicine.

B : In that case, I had better drive you home.

> A : 吃點藥後,我覺得昏昏沉沉。
>
> B : 在那種情況下,我最好開車送你回家。

 under the weather 身體不舒服

A : I feel under the weather. I ache all over.

B : I think you got the flu.

> A : 我覺得身體不舒服,全身疼痛。
>
> B : 我想你得了流感。

▶▶ **write out a prescription 開張藥方**

是開處方。

A: I'll write out a prescription for you. You have to remember to take these pills after meals.

B: What if I don't have an appetite?

A: 我給你開張藥方,你必須記住飯後要吃藥。

B: 萬一我沒胃口怎麼辦?

10 態度場景

▶▶ # be hard on sb. **對某人嚴厲**

A: I am punishing my son for trying to put paper clips into the electrical socket.

B: You shouldn't be too hard on him. He's only three and doesn't know any better.

A: 我在處罰我的兒子,因為他想放迴紋針進去電源插座裡面。

B: 你不應該對他太嚴厲,他只有3歲,而且還不懂事。

not know any better 不懂事。

▶▶ # be right behind sb. **支持某人**

A: I am considering running for the Academic Senate and I could really use your support.

B: Don't worry, Jack. No matter what, I'll be right behind you.

 ：我正在考慮競選學術委員，很需要你的支持。

B：傑克，不要擔心，不管怎樣，我都會支持你。

補充

could use 需要。

▶▶ **bet sb. is right** 同意某人的看法

A：Janice said that the test has been changed to this Friday, but I don't believe her.

B：I bet she's right!

 ：珍妮絲說，考試已經改到這星期五，但是我不相信她。

B：我相信她說的話！

▶▶ **give up** 放棄

解說

此片語後面要接名詞或動名詞。

A : If you work hard and never give up your dreams, you'll obtain what you want.

B : Thanks for the advice, Mom.

> **A** : 如果你很努力且不放棄你的夢想，你就會得到你想要的。
>
> **B** : 媽媽，謝謝你的建議。

▶▶ **go along with** 附和

A : I'll do the talking, and all you have to do is go along with it.

B : Ok, but I have a feeling that she's going to know we're lying.

> **A** : 我負責說話，而你所需要做的就是附和。
>
> **B** : 好的，但是我有一種感覺，她會知道我們在說謊。

 補充

do the＋v-ing，表示做某件事，如 do the talking 負責說話，do the cooking 煮飯，do the eating 吃東西，do the shopping 購物。

▶▶ grant sb.'s request 同意某人的請求

A: So, are you going to Las Vegas with us?

B: Yes. I asked my boss for the time off, and he granted my request.

A: 所以,你會跟我們去拉斯維加斯嗎?

B: 會啊,我要求我老闆放我假,而他同意我的請求。

▶▶ itch for 渴望

A: I haven't taken time off in over 2 years.

B: You must be itching for a vacation.

A: 在過去兩年內,我都沒放假。

B: 你一定渴望一個假期。

▶▶ live with oneself 心安理得

解說

不會感到內疚，多用於否定句中。

A : I dropped 10 grand on the blackjack tables last week.

B : How could you live with yourself ?

A : 上週我在二十一點的賭桌上輸了一萬美元。

B : 你怎麼能心安理得呢？

▶▶ look up to sb. 尊敬

A : Who in your life do you look up to the most?

B : Actually, I have always admired my dad.

A : 你一生之中，最尊敬誰呢？

B : 事實上，我一向很尊敬我的父親。

▶▶ low profile 低調

 I think we should try to keep a low profile until things calm down.

 Yes. Keeping a low profile is always a good idea.

> 我想我們應該保持低調直到事情平靜下來為止。
>
> 沒錯,保持低調總是個好主意。

補充

calm down 平靜下來,high profile 高調。

▶▶ side with sb. 支持某人

解說

指與某人抱持同樣的見解。

 I think the teacher will side with me, not to give a final.

 I doubt it. The teacher is required by the school to give a final.

A: 我想老師會支持我，不會舉行期末考。

B: 我不相信，學校會要求教師舉行期末考。

▶▶ **stand up for** 支持

A: Who will you stand up for?

B: I'm with you.

A: 你會支持誰？

B: 我支持你。

PART

第 **3** 單元

類似片語

3

 PART

01 贊成場景

▶▶ # And how! 當然

A : Do you think Professor White's test is too difficult?

B : And how!

> **A** : 你認為懷特教授的測驗很困難嗎？
>
> **B** : 當然很困難。

▶▶ # I see eye to eye with you.
我同意你的看法

指意見、觀念或看法一致；而 see eye to eye 為「有相同的看法」的意思。

A : We should do some serious shopping before Christmas because everything is on sale.

B : I see eye to eye with you.

A : 我們應該在聖誕節之前做大採購，因為每樣東西都在特價。

B : 我同意你的看法。

▶▶ You can say that again. 你說得很對

A : It is a pity that you didn't win the final match.

B : You can say that again.

A : 真可惜，你沒贏得最後決賽。

B : 你說得很對。

▶▶ You said it. 你說得很對

A : The teacher's lecture is fascinating.

B : You said it.

A : 老師的演講很棒。

B : 你說得很對。

贊成的類似說法還有 by all means.（當然可以）、You bet.（當然）、It couldn't be better.（再好不過了）、I couldn't agree more.（我完全同意）、Sure thing.（當然）、I don't doubt it.（我相信）。

02 反對場景

▶▶ Are you kidding? 你在開玩笑嗎

A: Could you give the note to Betty.

B: Are you kidding? Can't you see I'm busy?

A: 你能把筆記交給貝蒂嗎？
B: 你在開玩笑嗎？你沒看見我正在忙嗎？

▶▶ Don't look at me. 別看我

A: I want to buy that black backpack but I am about 10 dollars short.

B: Don't look at me. I have no money.

A: 我想要買那黑色的後背包，但是我缺10美元。
B: 別看我，我沒錢。

▶▶ I couldn't agree less. 我完全不同意

A: That junk food tastes good.

B: To tell the truth, I couldn't agree less.

A: 那速食味道不錯。

B: 說實話，我完全不同意。

▶▶ Who says so? 誰說的

A: The new opera is fantastic.

B: Who says so? I can't believe that.

A: 這新的歌劇很棒。

B: 誰說的？我才不相信。

補充

在西方語言表達過程中，若不直接回應面對的問題時，則表示有反對的意思，其類似的說法還有 I don't know about that.（我不知道這一點）、You must be kidding.（你一定在開玩笑）。

(03) 完成場景

▶▶ **be done (with)** 做完

A : Are you finally done with your papers?

B : I'm finished.

A : 你終於做完你的報告了嗎？
B : 我做完了。

▶▶ **be finished (with)** 做完

A : I am finished with my dissertation. And I will have my oral next week.

B : I believe you can pass the oral.

A : 我做完我的博士論文，而我下週要進行口試。
B : 我相信你可以通過口試。

▶▶ be through (with) 做完

A : I have to hand in the paper before Friday.

B : By then, I'll be through with it, too.

A : 我在星期五前必須繳交這份報告。

B : 到那時，我也做完了。

04 健忘場景

▶▶ absent-minded 心不在焉

A : I was so absent-minded that I forgot my pen.

B : Never mind. I can lend you one.

A : 我真是心不在焉，竟然忘了帶筆。
B : 沒關係，我可以借你一枝。

▶▶ have a short memory 記性不好

A : I have forgotten your sister's birthday. I have a short memory.

B : I'll remind you next time.

A : 我忘了你妹妹的生日，我的記性不好。
B : 下次我會提醒你。

▶▶ slip sb.'s mind 忘記

A : Do you know when we should hand in the report?

B : Sorry, it slipped my mind.

> **A** : 你知道我們應該何時繳交報告嗎?
>
> **B** : 抱歉,我忘記了。

 明白場景

▶▶ **catch on** 理解

catch on 以人爲主詞時，意思爲「理解」的意思，而以物爲主詞時，爲「流行」的意思。

A: I don't like that kind of abstract painting. I can't catch on the meaning of it.

B: It makes more sense the second time.

A: 我不喜歡那一類的抽象畫，我不能理解畫中的含意。

B: 看第二次就會比較理解了。

▶▶ **make any sense out of** 明白

A: Could you make any sense out of what I said?

B: I didn't quite catch on what you said just now.

A：你能明白我說的話嗎？

B：我不太懂你剛才說的內容。

▶▶ make heads or tails of 明白

A：I can't make heads or tails of how to put that into English.

B：It's above me.

A：我不能明白如何把它翻譯成英語。

B：它超乎我能力之所及。

06 厭倦場景

▶▶ **be fed up with** 厭倦

A : I am fed up with watching soap operas every night.

B : You are right. It wastes so a lot of time.

> A : 我厭倦每晚看肥皂劇。
>
> B : 你說得很對，它浪費很多時間。

▶▶ **be sick of** 厭倦

A : I am sick of doing the same thing over and over again.

B : Me, too.

> A : 我厭倦一再地做相同的事。
>
> B : 我也一樣。

▶▶ **be tired of** 對…厭煩

A ⁚ The fall is over. The winter is coming.

B ⁚ I'm tired of the winter. I hope the winter will soon be over.

A ⁚ 秋天結束，冬天來臨了。

B ⁚ 我對冬天感到厭煩，希望冬天很快就會過去。

07 做事困難場景

▶▶ have a hard time doing 做…有困難

A: The report is due tomorrow. Could you work on it with me tonight?

B: Unfortunately, I have a hard time writing it.

> **A:** 報告明天要交,今晚你能跟我一起做這份報告嗎?
>
> **B:** 很不幸地,寫這份報告對我來說有困難。

▶▶ have a problem doing 做…有困難

A: I have a problem getting through the book.

B: By all means. It will take you a lot of time to work on it.

> **A:** 看完這本書對我來說是一大挑戰。
>
> **B:** 沒錯,你需要花費很多時間讀它。

▶▶ have difficulty doing 做…有困難

A : Are you through with your report?

B : I have difficulty writing it.

> **A** : 你的報告完成了嗎？
>
> **B** : 這份報告很難寫。

▶▶ have trouble doing 做…有困難

A : I have trouble writing the essay.

B : Why don't you ask Joy?

> **A** : 我在寫短文時遭遇困難。
>
> **B** : 你為什麼不請教喬伊呢？

08 抱怨場景

▶▶ be not worth 不值

指沒有那個價值。

A: I decided to buy that furniture.

B: It is very old and it is not worth the money.

A: 我決定買那件家具。

B: 家具很舊，不值那些錢。

▶▶ drive sb. crazy 讓某人發瘋

A: It's too much for me. The noise next door drives me crazy.

B: It's more than I can bear, too.

A: 我受不了，隔壁鄰居的噪音讓我發瘋。

B: 我也一樣受不了。

▶▶ It never fails 從來都是這樣

A : It never fails. He plays this trick on me on Halloween.

B : That happened to me once.

A : 從來都是這樣，他每逢萬聖節就捉弄我。

B : 這種事情也曾經發生在我身上。

PART

09 故障場景

▶▶ be down 故障

A : The iPad is down. I have to send it to be repaired.

B : You can take it to Otto's repair shop. They are pretty reasonable.

> **A** : iPad 故障了，我必須送修。
>
> **B** : 你可以帶它去奧托的維修店裡，他們價錢很合理。

▶▶ break down 故障

A : Hi, I see you walking. Where is your car today?

B : My car broke down yesterday, so I had to take it to the car repair shop.

> **A** : 嗨，我看見你在走路。今天你的車子呢？
>
> **B** : 我的車子昨天故障了，所以我必須把它送去汽車維修廠。

223

▶▶ conk out 故障

指機器或車輛停止運轉。

A: My washer finally conked out on me. It looks like I'm going to have to buy a new one.

B: Well, you couldn't expect it to run forever.

A: 我的洗衣機終於故障了,看起來我好像得買一台新的了。

B: 嗯,你不能期待它可以永遠運轉。

▶▶ doesn't work 故障

A: Your computer is slow. It is about seven years old.

B: It's only a matter of time before my computer doesn't work.

A: 你的電腦速度很慢,用了大約有7年了。

B: 我的電腦遲早會故障,只是時間問題。

故障的類似說法還有 out of order（故障）、be done for（用壞了）、go haywire（失靈）。

▶▶ on the blink 故障

用在機器、儀表板的故障。

A : I need to type a resume now. Could I use your laptop?

B : I'd love to, but sadly, it's on the blink.

> A : 我現在需要打一份履歷，我可以使用你的筆記型電腦嗎？
>
> B : 我很願意，但是很慘的是它故障了。

PART

10 弄錯場景

 get confused 弄混淆

解說

指糊塗或迷惑不解。

A : Why were you not at the meeting last night?

B : I got confused. I thought the meeting is tonight.

A : 你為什麼昨晚沒來開會？

B : 我弄混淆了，我以為是今晚要開會。

mistake for 把…誤認為

A : The biology paper's deadline is tomorrow.

B : That's too bad. I mistook the due date for next Friday.

A : 明天是生物報告截止日期。

B : 那太糟糕了，我把到期日誤認為下星期五。

▶▶ **mix up** 弄錯

指弄混淆或弄錯。

A: I'm very upset. I mixed up the time of my yoga class yesterday.

B: I think you weren't the only one.

A: 我很沮喪，我昨天弄錯了瑜珈課的時間。

B: 我想你不是唯一弄錯的人。

11 一樣場景

▶▶ # It makes no difference to me.

這對我都一樣

A: The paper's deadline has been extended to three days later.

B: It makes no difference to me.

A: 這份報告已經延期到三天後。

B: 這對我都一樣。

▶▶ # It's all the same to me. 這對我都一樣

A: Would you like to eat out or eat at home to-night?

B: It's all the same to me.

A: 你今晚想在外面吃或在家吃呢？

B: 這對我都一樣。

▶▶ It doesn't make any difference to me. 這對我都一樣

A : The get-together has been changed from Saturday to Sunday.

B : It doesn't make any difference to me.

A : 聚會已從星期六改為星期日。

B : 這對我都一樣。

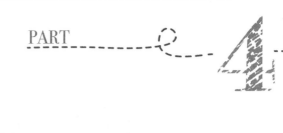

第 **4** 單元

必備片語

PART

▶▶ a freak of nature 畸形

解說

用在描述動物、植物或昆蟲長的很奇特。

A : Have you seen what an Amazonian cockroach looks like?

B : Yeah, and what a freak of nature it is.

A : 你有沒有看過亞馬遜蟑螂的長相？
B : 有，它非常畸形。

▶▶ a little something 小東西

解說

小東西，通常是用來表示對某人的謝意。

A : Ok, dad. I'm off to school.

B : Check the table before you go. I left you a little something.

：好的，爸爸，我要去學校了。

：你走以前，看一下桌上，我給你留了小東西。

▶▶ act like clowns 行為很愚蠢

【解說】

行為像小丑，表示很愚蠢或常失態； 若此片語中，主詞是單數，則為 act like a clown。

：Whenever Jim and Eric get together, they are always acting like clowns.

：Yeah, they never want to take things seriously.

：每當吉姆和艾利克在一起時，他們總是做些很愚蠢的行為。

：對啊，他們從不想認真地處事。

【補充】

take seriously 認真對待，act like a clown = to act silly / stupid / crazy

▶▶ all over the place 到處

A: I've been looking all over the place, but I can't find where my dog is.

B: Have you called the pound? Maybe someone took her there.

> **A**: 我一直在到處的尋找,但是我就是找不到我的狗。
>
> **B**: 你有打電話給動物收容所嗎?或許有人帶牠去那裡。

▶▶ an odd couple 不匹配

直譯為「一對奇怪的情侶」,引申為「不匹配」或「不合適」。

A: Do you think Mr. and Mrs. Smith are a bit of an odd couple?

B: Well, they are both very strange, so I think they make a perfect match.

：你認為史密斯先生和太太有一點不匹配嗎？

B：嗯，他們倆都很奇怪，所以我想他們很相配。

▶▶ as sb. see fit 適合的

解說

意思爲某人覺得適合，強調可按照自己意思行事。

A：Brian, I want you going to U.C. Berkeley like your father did.

B：Mom, I am a grown man now, and I will make my own choices as I see fit.

：布萊恩，我希望你像你父親一樣，去讀加州伯克萊大學。

B：媽媽，我現在是成年人，我會做出適合自己的選擇。

補充

see fit 認爲適當。

at the mercy of 受…擺布

A: Human beings are on the top of the food chain.

B: Yeah, but when you go camping in the woods, you are at the mercy of the bears.

> **A:** 人類位在食物鏈的上層。
>
> **B:** 沒錯,但是當你去森林裡露營時,你的存活取決於熊是否出沒。

be angry at sb. 對某人生氣

A: How did you do at your football tryouts?

B: The coach was angry at me when I missed a simple tackle.

> **A:** 你的足球選拔賽結果怎麼樣?
>
> **B:** 我錯失了簡單的阻截,教練對我很生氣。

▶▶ be caught red-handed 被當場抓住

指犯罪時被當場抓住。

A : Why was John arrested?

B : He was caught red- handed, stealing beer from the supermarket.

A : 約翰為什麼被逮捕呢？

B : 他偷超級市場的啤酒被當場抓住。

▶▶ be like trying to find a flea on an elephant's ass 很困難

就像在大象屁股上找一隻跳蚤般困難，形容一件事情很難。

A : There will be 40,000 people at the concert. Finding you will be like trying to find a flea on an elephant's ass.

B：We'll meet outside the entrance an hour before the show.

A：音樂會會有40,000人，找你會很困難。

B：在表演開始前一小時，我們在入口外面碰頭。

▶▶ be jammed with 擠滿

A：You'd better show up to class early during the first week.

B：Yeah, I know the classes are usually jammed with students trying to add, during the first week of the semester.

A：開學第一週，你最好早點來上課。

B：好的，我知道在學期的第一週，教室裡經常擠滿了想要加選的學生。

▶▶ all set 準備好了

A：Are you all set?

B：No, I still need to comb my hair.

A ：你準備好了嗎？

B ：還沒，我還需要梳頭髮。

▶▶ always the case 總是如此

A ：He's cooking up a story to explain why he was late. I can't stand it any longer.

B ：It's always the case with him. You'll get used to it soon.

A ：他正在編故事來解釋他為什麼遲到，我再也無法忍受了。

B ：他總是如此，你很快就會習慣了。

▶▶ as a whole 整體來看

A ：How did I do on my midterm?

B ：As a whole, you improved considerably.

A ：我期中考試考得如何？

B ：整體來看，你有了顯著的進步。

▶▶ Are you saying that...? 你是說…嗎

指用在確認對方講話內容時。

A: The boat capsized nearly three days ago, and we haven't found a trace of any survivors.

B: Are you saying that you're going to call off the search?

A: 約在3天前,小船翻覆了,而我們還沒有找到任何生還者的蹤跡。

B: 你是說你將要停止搜尋了嗎?

▶▶ be a far cry from 大不相同

A: How is your thesis coming along?

B: The thesis is a far cry from the original one three months ago.

A: 你的論文進展的如何?

B: 三個月前的初稿和現在的論文是大不相同。

▶▶ be behind in 拖延

A : I think the teacher will lower my grade because I was behind in my assignment.

B : Absolutely right.

> **A** : 我想因為我作業遲交，老師會降低我的成績。
> **B** : 完全正確。

▶▶ be beset with 被…包圍

A : Bush wants to run for student government again. What do you think of it?

B : I think his situation is bad. He is beset with scandals right now.

> **A** : 布希想要再競選學生會，你認為怎麼樣呢？
> **B** : 我想他的情況不好，他目前被醜聞所包圍。

▶▶ be disgusted with 厭惡

A: I am disgusted with people using animals to test drugs on.

B: Me, too. I think what scientists and doctors do to animals is cruel and inhumane.

> **A:** 我厭惡人類用動物來測試藥物。
>
> **B:** 我也是,我想科學家和醫生對動物所做的事是殘酷與不人道的。

▶▶ be dying to 渴望

A: I'm dying to know if I aced the exam.

B: So am I, but the secretary is not authorized to tell you.

> **A:** 我渴望知道我是否高分通過考試。
>
> **B:** 我也一樣想知道,但祕書沒有權力告知你。

▶▶ be left wide open 留下大空檔

A : Why didn't you pass the ball? I was left wide open.

B : Sorry. I was being double covered, and didn't see you.

> **A** : 你為什麼沒傳球？我這邊是大空檔。
> **B** : 抱歉，我被兩人防守，而沒看到你。

▶▶ be tagged 被逮住

A : Why didn't you meet us at the park last night?

B : I was tagged by my parents, trying to sneak out.

> **A** : 你昨晚為什麼沒有在公園跟我們會面呢？
> **B** : 我想偷溜出去但被我父母逮住了。

be tagged = be caught

▶▶ beat sb. to the punch
比某人搶先一步

A: I wanted to ask Michelle to the dance, but Jim beat me to the punch.

B: There will be other dances to come.

> **A**: 我想要邀蜜雪兒跳舞,但是吉姆搶先一步。
>
> **B**: 肯定還會有別的舞會。

▶▶ bent out of shape 氣壞了

A: I'm just joking. You don't need to get bent out of shape over it.

B: Whether you're joking or not, I don't think jokes about my mom are funny.

> **A**: 我只是開個玩笑啦,你不需要為這件事氣壞了。
>
> **B**: 不管你是否在開玩笑,我不認為關於我媽媽的玩笑話好笑。

▶▶ bigger fish to fry 更重要的事情要辦

解說

有更大的魚要炸，引申有更重要的事要辦。

A'：Have you been studying for the midterm tomorrow?

B'：I have bigger fish to fry, like studying for the SAT test on Saturday.

A'：你有為明天期中考試準備嗎？

B'：我有更重要的事情要辦，像準備星期六的 SAT 考試。

▶▶ black and blue 遍體鱗傷

A'：What's the matter with you? You look black and blue.

B'：I fell down the stairs.

A'：你怎麼了？你看起來遍體鱗傷。

B'：我從樓梯上摔了下來。

▶▶ blow sb. away 徹底擊敗對方

 解說

在比賽情境中，blow sb. away 強調徹底擊垮對方；而 blow sth. away 有「把東西吹走」的意思，如 The wind blew my hat away. 風吹走我的帽子。

> **A** : The Red Sox blew the Yankees away in the World Series this past year.

> **B** : You can say that again. The curse on the Red Sox has finally been lifted.

> **A** : 在過去這一年，紅襪隊在世界棒球大賽把洋基隊徹底擊敗了。
>
> **B** : 你說對了，紅襪隊的詛咒終於解除了。

▶▶ boil down to 結果是

 解說

有「意味著」、「歸結為」、「重點是」或「結果是」的意思。

> **A** : So, what does this boil down to?

B : If you don't get at least a 90 on your next test, you will fail the course.

A : 所以，結果是什麼呢？

B : 如果下次考試，你沒有到達90分以上，這門課就會不及格。

▶▶ bring sb. around 把某人帶來

A : I'm sorry things got out of hand last night. I won't bring Eric around anymore.

B : Yeah, that guy has a serious temper problem when he drinks.

A : 對不起，昨晚情況失控，我再也不會帶艾利克來了。

B : 對啊，那傢伙喝酒脾氣就會變得很壞。

▶▶ break loose 掙脫

A : My dog broke loose from his chain, and escaped.

B : Let's split up, and go looking for him.

> **A** : 我的狗從鏈子上掙脫逃跑了。
>
> **B** : 讓我們分頭去找牠。

▶▶ break sth. in 磨合

break sth. in 是指物的磨合，強調要經常的使用，使它逐漸合用；而 break sb. in 是指人為幫助某人適應某事。

A : My baseball glove is really stiff.

B : They're all new. It will take about a week for you to break it in.

> **A** : 我的棒球手套很硬。
>
> **B** : 它們是全新的，你需要花大約一週的時間來磨合。

248

▶▶ buddy up with sb. 交朋友

buddy 在口語中是「好朋友」的意思，在當動詞用時爲「交朋
友」。

A : The best way to pass his class is to buddy up with someone and study together.

B : I already made arrangements to study with Nick.

A : 要通過他的課最好的方式是找個好朋友一起學習。

B : 我已經跟尼克約好一起唸書了。

▶▶ by fair means or foul 不擇手段

A : I heard you didn't pass the midterm.

B : Sure. So I have to get high scores in the final exam, by fair means or foul.

A : 我聽說你沒通過期中考。

B : 沒錯，所以我必須不擇手段在期末考中取得高分。

▶▶ by hook or by crook 不擇手段

解說

有「想盡辦法」、「不擇手段」、「千方百計」的意思。

A: He intends to win a scholarship to Cambridge University. And he'll do it by hook or by crook.

B: If he hits the books, he will get it.

A: 他打算爭取劍橋大學獎學金，而他會不擇手段爭取它。

B: 如果他用功讀書，就會得到獎學金。

補充

by hook or by crook = by crook = by hook or crook

▶▶ can't stand it any longer
再也不能忍受了

A: Can you believe the professor asked us to turn in a thirty-page report in two weeks?

B: I feel this course is too hard. I can't stand it any longer.

> A：你能相信教授要我們在兩週內繳交30頁的報告嗎？
>
> B：我覺得這課程太難，我再也不能忍受了。

▶▶ catch-22 令人左右為難的處境

置身於左右為難的處境，而自身無法脫離此困境。

> A：I have two tests to study for, and don't know where to begin.
>
> B：Sounds like a catch-22.

> A：我有2個考試要準備，而我不知道從何開始。
>
> B：聽起來像是令人左右為難的處境。

▶▶ chap sb.'s hide 讓某人感到頭疼

指讓人討厭或心煩。

A: The professor's methods of teaching really chap my hide.

B: Yeah, he makes the material so difficult to understand.

A: 這位教授的教學方法真的讓我感到頭疼。

B: 是啊,他讓教材變的很難理解。

▶▶ **come for sb.** 來接(某人)

此片語後面若接物,為「come for sth.來取某物」,如 I'll come for the photos tomorrow. 我明天會來取相片。

A: We are lost in the middle of the woods, and our compass doesn't work.

B: We need to stay calm. Someone will come for us.

A: 我們迷失在森林的深處,而且指南針故障了。

B: 我們需要保持冷靜,有人會來接我們的。

PART

▶▶ come in handy 派上用場

針對某種目的，遲早會用到。

A: I am going to clean out my room today, and throw away all the junk I don't use anymore.

B: You should hold on to your stuffed animals because they may come in handy once you have kids.

A: 我今天會把我的房間打掃乾淨，扔掉所有我不再使用的垃圾。

B: 你應該保留填充玩偶，因為一旦你有小孩，它們可能會派上用場。

clean out 打掃乾淨；throw away 扔掉；hold on to 保留。

253

PART

▶▶ come up 發生

強調沒有想到，突然間發生。

 : I was supposed to return your notes yesterday, but something had come up.

B : It doesn't matter. I will pick it up by Friday.

A : 我昨天應該歸還你的筆記，可是發生了一些事。

B : 沒關係，在星期五前，我會過來拿。

▶▶ complete with 附有

強調包括在主體裡面。

 : I turned in the report, complete with supporting documents.

B : You should expect a good grade then.

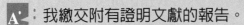

A : 我繳交附有證明文獻的報告。

B : 那麼你應該會拿到一個好成績。

▶▶ **count on sb.** 指望某人

指依靠或指望某人。

A : I can always count on my mom to be there for me when I'm feeling depressed.

B : Yeah, mom's the best.

A : 當我覺得沮喪時，總是可以指望我媽媽，她總會陪伴著我。

B : 沒錯，媽媽是最棒的。

▶▶ **cut it close** 幾乎來不及

是說來不及完成事情，造成時間上很緊張。

A : I am going to start studying on Friday for our final.

B : Don't you think that's cutting it close? The test is going to be on Monday.

A : 我星期五要開始準備期末考試。

B : 你不認為那樣幾乎會來不及嗎？這考試是在星期一舉行。

▶▶ date back to 追溯到

A : Look at the painting. It must date back to the Renaissance.

B : Well, that's great. Whose work do you think it is?

A : 看看這幅畫，它八成可以追溯到文藝復興時代。

B : 嗯，不錯，你認為它是誰的作品？

date back to = derive from

▶▶ deep down 說真的

來自心中眞實的感覺。

A: Deep down I know we're right for each other, but I don't know if I am ready to get married yet.

B: Well, if she truly loves you, she will wait until you are ready.

A: 說真的,我知道我們很適合對方,但是我不知道我是否準備好要結婚了。

B: 嗯,如果她真的愛你,她會等你做好準備。

補充
get married 結婚。

▶▶ die down 冷清

指變得越來越弱,直到消失爲止,也就是漸漸散去,而在此宴會情境中,翻譯爲「冷清」。

A: This party is beginning to die down.

B: Do you want to go to a dance club instead?

：這舞會開始冷清了。

 ：你想要去別家舞廳嗎？

▶▶ do the honors （很榮幸）幫忙

解說
本身是幫忙的意思，但是這幫忙帶有很榮幸的意思。

 ：Would you like to do the honors and say grace?

 ：I'm sorry, but I am not Christian.

 ：你願意幫忙做謝恩禱告嗎？

 ：對不起，我不是基督徒。

▶▶ drop everything 擱下一切

解說
要放下手中的事情來做某事。

A : In the event of an earthquake, you are to drop everything and hide under your desk.

B : That would be cool to have an earthquake at school. Then we'd get to go home early.

A : 一旦發生地震,你要擱下一切,躲到桌子底下。

B : 上課時發生地震很棒,這樣我們就能提早回家。

▶▶ **drop out of 休學**

指從什麼當中退出,也就是「不參與」或「退出」的意思,而用在學校情境中,指「休學」。

A : I think I might fail all the courses. I will be dropping out of college.

B : Try to look on the bright side of things. You still have three weeks to prepare for them.

A : 我想我可能所有課程都不及格,我將會休學。

B : 儘量朝正面想,你還有三週的時間來準備考試。

▶▶ dry out 變乾

A: I can't use regular soap because it dries my skin out too much.

B: It probably contains too many chemicals.

> **A:** 我不能使用一般肥皂,因為我的皮膚會變得非常乾燥。
>
> **B:** 它可能含有太多的化學物質。

▶▶ dwell on 老是想著

強調一再地思考某事,也就是「老是想著」某事的意思。

A: I can't stop thinking about the midterm I failed.

B: Stop dwelling on the past, and you need to prepare harder for the final.

> **A:** 我沒辦法不去想我期中考不及格的事。
>
> **B:** 不要老是想著過去的事,你需要更努力準備期末考。

補充

stop thinking about 不要再想。

▶▶ extend sb.'s sympathy 表達哀悼

解說

表達同情、慰問或哀悼。

A: Hey, Kevin. I just stopped by to extend my sympathies for the loss of your father. Let me know if there is anything I can do for you.

B: Thanks, Susan. I think I just want to be alone right now.

A: 嗨，凱文，對於你父親的去世，我過來表達哀悼，如果有什麼事需要我幫忙的話，讓我知道。

B: 謝謝，蘇珊，我想我現在只想要獨處。

▶▶ fall down 跌倒

A: I hate skating because I fall down on the snow.

B: You'll learn it after a few days.

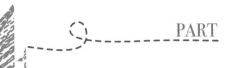

A：因為我在雪上跌倒，我討厭滑雪。

B：幾天之後，你就會學會。

▶▶ far from 完全不是

A：I can't understand the meaning of painting.

B：It's far from my favorite kind of painting.

A：我不能理解這幅畫的意義。

B：它完全不是我最喜歡的那種畫。

▶▶ fair and square 光明正大

A：I believe you cheated, so I am not going to pay you.

B：We won that game fair and square, and deserve our winnings.

A：我認為你作弊，所以不會給你獎金。

B：我們光明正大贏得那比賽，我們應得到獎金。

▶▶ follow in sb.'s footsteps
跟隨某人的腳步

A : Do you plan to follow in your father's footsteps as a teacher?

B : I don't think I'd be a good teacher.

A : 你有計畫要跟隨你父親的腳步當一位老師嗎？

B : 我想我不會是一位好老師。

▶▶ from the look of sb.
從某人的外表看來

A : From the look of you, I'd say you have a fever.

B : I think so, too. I feel dizzy now.

A : 從你的外表來看，我認為你感冒了。

B : 我也這樣認為，我現在覺得頭暈。

▶▶ gang up on sb. 聯合起來對付某人

A: You have to do your chores and homework, or you cannot go out.

B: Why do you always have to gang up on me?

> **A:** 你必須做家事和作業，否則你不能出去。
>
> **B:** 你們為什麼總是要聯合起來對付我呢？

▶▶ get at 意思

指「暗示」、「意指」或「意思」。

A: I don't know what you're getting at?

B: I mean that the Amazon is the world's largest tropical rainforest.

> **A:** 我不知道你的意思是什麼？
>
> **B:** 我的意思是亞馬遜河是世界上最大的熱帶雨林。

▶▶ **get back** 恢復

強調恢復到原來的狀況；此片語也有「回來」的意思，如 I sleep over there and get back on Sunday.我在那裡過夜，在星期日回來。

A : I heard you broke up with your girlfriend of seven years.

B : Yes. It's going to take a long time for everything to get back to normal.

A : 我聽說你跟交往7年的女友分手了。

B : 沒錯，想要一切生活都恢復正常，需要很長時間。

▶▶ **get in** 進入

A : The admission price to the museum is eight bucks per person. I feel it's hardly worth that much.

B : But we get in for three with the student card.

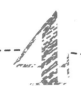

> **A:** 博物館的門票是每人八塊錢，我覺得它不值得那麼多錢。
>
> **B:** 但是我們買學生票進入只要三塊錢。

▶▶ get lost 迷路

A: I remember I got lost in the woods one time and I was scared to death.

B: To be honest, I don't buy your story because you are a sophisticated hunter.

> **A:** 我記得有一次在森林裡迷路，我害怕的要死。
>
> **B:** 老實說，我不相信你的話，因為你是一個老練的獵人。

▶▶ get off the hook 擺脫麻煩

A: Do you want to go with us to the baseball game tomorrow?

B: I told my mom I'd babysit my little sister tomorrow, but I'll see if I can get off the hook.

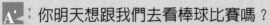

> **A** ：你明天想跟我們去看棒球比賽嗎？
>
> **B** ：我告訴我媽媽，明天我會看顧我的妹妹，不過說不定我能擺脫麻煩。

▶▶ get out of hand 難以控制

A ：I do not want to babysit your kids anymore.

B ：Why? Are they beginning to get out of hand?

> **A** ：我不想再看顧你的小孩。
>
> **B** ：為什麼呢？他們開始變得難以控制了嗎？

▶▶ get over it 忘掉過去

指忘卻過去，恢復平靜的情緒。

A ：I haven't been sleeping well lately. I cannot stop thinking about Ashley.

B ：It has been three months since she broke up with you. Don't you think it's time to get over it?

A：我最近一直沒睡好，我沒辦法不想艾希莉。

B：自從她跟你分手已經有3個月了，你不覺得是時候該忘掉過去了嗎？

▶▶ get the heck out of 趕緊離開

get out of 離開，the heck 是加強語氣。

A：There is another hurricane coming this way.

B：I'm getting the heck out of here this time.

A：有另一個颶風朝這方向來。

B：這一次我要趕緊離開這裡。

▶▶ give away the ending 說出結局

A：Have you seen the new Harry Potter movie yet?

B：No, and don't tell me anything. I don't want you to give away the ending like you did last time.

268

A : 你看過最新的哈利波特電影嗎？

B : 還沒有，不要告訴我任何事，我不想要你跟上次一樣說出結局。

▶▶ give it a rest 停下來

解說

是停下來做某事，以及對事情感到生氣或不耐煩。

A : Give it a rest already. I am not going to let you drive my car.

B : I'll let you ride my motorcycle, if you let me drive your car.

A : 先停下來，我不會讓你開我的車。

B : 如果你讓我開你的車，我會讓你騎我的摩托車。

▶▶ give it everything sb. got 竭盡全力

A : Try not to let us down, Peter. If we win this game, we'll go to the playoffs.

B : I'll give it everything I got.

4

> **A** : 彼得,不要讓我們失望,如果我們贏得這場比賽,就會進入決賽。
>
> **B** : 我會盡全力的。

▶▶ give sb. credit for 肯定某人

肯定或讚美某人的功勞、成就或行為。

A : I need to give my sister credit for the good grade in Algebra.

B : Did she help you with your homework a lot?

> **A** : 在代數上,我得肯定我妹妹成績優秀。
>
> **B** : 她有幫助你完成很多回家作業嗎?

▶▶ go down 發生

A : Is the bachelor party still scheduled to go down this Saturday?

B : Yeah, we are going to meet at Jim's house at 7:00 p.m.

A：這單身漢聚會還定在這星期六嗎？

B：是啊，晚上7點，我們會在吉姆家會面。

go down = happen

▶▶ **go into** 談論

指細談。

A：I'd love to talk to you about our relationship, but I don't have time to go into that right now.

B：That's why we never get along. You never make time to talk to me.

A：我的確想要跟你談談我們的關係，但是我現在沒有時間。

B：那也是為什麼我們無法和睦相處，你從來擠不出時間和我談話。

get along 和睦相處。

▶▶ **go on an errand for sb.** 為某人跑腿

指為某人辦事。

A: I need to discuss the play with you.

B: After going on an errand for my girlfriend, I'll meet you at the theatre.

A: 我需要跟你討論這劇本。

B: 在為我女友跑腿之後,我會在劇場和你見面。

go on an errand for sb. = run an errand for sb.

▶▶ go through 通過

常用在法律或政府協議有關的情境。

A: I lost my student card. What shall I do?

B: You must go through the proper channels to report its loss and to renew one.

A: 我遺失我的學生證，我該怎麼辦呢？

B: 你必須透過正當途徑來申報遺失並重新補發一張。

▶▶ gut feeling 預感

指直覺。

A: What makes you so sure that there is going to be a pop quiz today?

B: I am not totally sure. I just have a gut feeling.

A: 你憑什麼那樣肯定，今天會有隨堂考試呢？

B: 我不是十分確定，只是有預感。

▶▶ hack into 侵入

A: I heard Kevin hacked into the school computer and changed his grades.

B: Wow! If he gets caught, he will be expelled from school.

A: 我聽說凱文侵入學校的電腦，竄改他的成績。

B: 哇，如果他被逮到，他會被逐出學校。

▶▶ hand back 歸還

(解說)

指從某人手中借東西或拿東西，再歸還它們。

A: Are you going to hand back the test papers tomorrow?

B: I'm swamped with meetings, so I don't have them graded yet.

A：你明天會歸還試卷嗎？

B：我忙著開會，所以我還沒改完。

▶▶ hand down 傳給

指把某物傳下去。

A：How beautiful a bracelet it is. It will be envied by my friends.

B：My grandma handed it down to me as an heirloom.

A：多美麗的手鐲啊，它會讓我的朋友羨慕不已。

B：我祖母傳給我，作為傳家寶。

▶▶ hands-on 親自動手的

A：What do you think the best way to learn science is?

B：The best way to learn science is doing hands-on projects.

PART

A：你認為學習科學的最好方法是什麼？

B：學習科學的最好方法是親自動手做科研專題。

▶▶ hang on to sth. 緊緊握住某物

A：Let's go and walk the dog!

B：Hang on to the leash; otherwise we will have to chase the dog in the neighborhood.

A：讓我們去遛狗吧！

B：緊緊握住皮帶，否則我們得在附近追逐這隻狗。

▶▶ hard to believe 難以置信

指很難相信。

A：It's hard to believe that we are all getting married real soon.

B：I know. It seems like just yesterday we were 15 years old and preparing for high school.

：難以置信，很快，我們都要結婚。

 ：我知道，好像昨天我們都才15歲，正準備進入高中而已。

▶▶ have a crack at 試一試

 ：I hate algebra. I can't seem to figure out this question.

 ：Why don't you let me have a crack at it?

 ：我討厭代數，我似乎無法解出這個問題。

 ：你為什麼不讓我試一試？

▶▶ have a hunch 有預感

 ：I have a hunch that my girlfriend is going to get me a new MP3 player for Christmas.

 ：That would be awesome. I wish I had a boyfriend that would buy me things like that.

A : 我有預感，我的女朋友會在聖誕節買一台新的 MP3 播放機給我。

B : 那太棒了，我希望我有個會買那種東西給我的男朋友。

►► have a way with sth. 對某事有一套

用在人的方面，表示很能交際應酬；用在事情上，表示某人在某方面很有造詣。

A : I can always count on my mom to cheer me up when I am sad.

B : Me, too. Mothers have a way with words.

A : 當我傷心時，我媽媽的鼓勵總能讓我振作起來。

B : 我也是，媽媽們對鼓勵人很有一套。

▶▶ hotshot 老大

A: Bill Gates is the hotshot of the software industry.

B: It must be nice being the richest man in the world.

A: 比爾蓋茲是軟體工業的老大。

B: 身為世界上最富有的人，感覺一定很不錯。

▶▶ have sth. under control
某事在控制中

此片語也可寫成 get sth. under control，但較少用。

A: I am worried about all of the turbulence.

B: I'm sure the pilots have everything under control.

A: 我很擔心各種的亂流。

B: 我確信一切都在駕駛員的控制中。

have sth. out of control 某事不受控制。

▶▶ have the right to 有權

A: The police tried to get me to tell them about you. I told them I have the right to remain silent.

B: Thanks. I owe you one.

A: 警察設法逼我供出你,我告訴他們我有權保持緘默。

B: 謝謝,我欠你一個人情。

▶▶ head over heels 完全地

A: I heard you have been dating Betty.

B: Yes, to be frank with you, I'm head over heels in love with her.

A: 我聽說你最近在跟貝蒂約會。

B: 沒錯,坦白跟你說,我完全地落入她的情網。

▶▶ # hold on to 保存

指經過長時間的保存。

A：Do you want to sell some of your textbooks from last term?

B：I always hold on to them for future reference.

A：你想要賣一些上學期的教科書嗎？

B：我總是保存它們，以便將來作為參考。

▶▶ # hold still 靜止不動

A：Can you hold the cat still, while I clip its nails?

B：Sure. Just make sure it doesn't claw me.

A：當我幫貓剪指甲時，你能讓牠靜止不動嗎？

B：可以，只要你保證牠不會抓傷我。

PART

補充

hold still = keep still

▶▶ **I don't mean to** 我不是故意要

解說

此句型直譯為「我不是故意要」或「我無意」。

A: I don't mean to burst your bubble, but Santa Claus doesn't exist.

B: What are you talking about? I saw him eating cookies in my kitchen last Christmas.

A: 我不是故意要打碎你的幻想,但是聖誕老人並不存在。

B: 你在說些什麼?我去年聖誕節看見他在我的廚房裡吃餅乾。

PART

▶▶ in sb.'s shoes 處於某人的角度

解說

使處於某人的狀況、立場、處境與角度來思考。

 : Put yourself in my shoes. Would you trust Jeff with your car?

B : Probably not. I have a nice Mercedes, and he has an old Toyota.

 : 你站在我的角度想一想，你會放心把你的車子交給傑夫開嗎？

B : 大概不會，我擁有一台好的賓士，而他擁有一台老的豐田汽車。

補充

in sb.'s shoes = in sb.'s situation

283

▶▶ **in plain sight** 在顯眼的地方

強調在很容易看見的地方或在某人眼前。

A : How did you get caught cheating?

B : I made a mistake and left my cheat sheet in plain sight.

A : 你怎麼會作弊被抓到呢？

B : 我犯了一個錯誤，在顯眼的地方留下我的小抄。

▶▶ **jump in with both feet** 就去做

強調做任何事之前不曾想太多，就放手去做。

A : I am too afraid to ask Judy to the prom.

B : Sometimes you just need to take a risk, and jump in with both feet. The worst that can happen is that she'll say no.

：我是太害怕而不敢邀請茱蒂參加舞會。

B ：有時候你必須冒險，就放手去做，最壞的事也不過就是她拒絕你。

補 充

take a risk 冒險。

▶▶ **just go for it** 放手去做

A ：I want to apply to Harvard, but it is so hard to get accepted.

B ：Why don't you just go for it? You have nothing to lose, but the time it takes you to fill out the application.

 ：我要申請哈佛大學，但是很難錄取。

B ：你為什麼不放手去做呢？你沒有什麼好損失的，除了要花時間填寫申請文件。

補 充

fill out 填寫。

▶▶ keep on top 掌控

指能保持某種的優勢。

A : I put at least two hours each night at the library, just so that I can keep on top of my studies.

B : It sounds to me like you are enrolled in too many classes.

A : 我每晚至少花2小時在圖書館裡，以便掌控我的學習。

B : 聽起來，你好像選了太多課。

▶▶ keep up with 跟上

A : How are you getting along with your physics studies?

B : There is so much to learn, but I am able to keep up with my classmates.

A：你的物理學得怎樣呢？

B：要學的東西很多，但是我可以跟上我同學的學習進度。

▶▶ knock it off 停下來

A：Knock it off, Sam; I'm trying to do my homework.

B：Fine, I'll go into the other room then.

A：山姆，停下來，我在做回家作業。

B：好的，那麼我會去其他的房間。

▶▶ know the score 心裡有數

A：You know the score, no playing cards until your homework is done.

B：I finished my homework at school today.

A：你心裡有數，作業沒做完前是不准打牌。

B：我今天在學校就把家庭作業做完了。

PART

▶▶ let go of 放棄

解說
指不再擁有某物，有「放開」、「放下」、「鬆開」、「放棄」的意思。

A：Why did you change your major?

B：I let go of my dream of becoming a teacher, and decided to be an artist instead.

A：你為什麼要改變自己的主修科目呢？

B：我放棄當老師的夢想，決定改當一名藝術家。

▶▶ lift the ban 解禁

A：I heard the barking of a dog last night, so I could hardly sleep.

B：You mean your dorm lifted the ban on dogs.

A：我昨晚聽到狗叫聲，所以我簡直無法入眠。

B：你的意思是說，宿舍禁養狗的規定解除了。

288

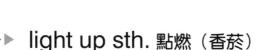

▶▶ light up sth. 點燃（香菸）

A：I like to light up a cigarette after eating.

B：You should try to quit it before you get lung cancer.

> **A**：吃完飯後，我喜歡來一根菸。
> **B**：在你得肺癌之前，你應該要努力戒菸。

▶▶ look out 照顧

A：Your parents have looked out for you for a long time. Don't you think it's time to give them a break?

B：As soon as I save enough money, I will move out.

> **A**：你的父母已經照顧你一段很長的時間了，你不覺得該是給他們休息的時候了嗎？
> **B**：我一存夠錢，就會搬出去。

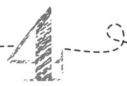

▶▶ look up 查詢

 : I do not know the meaning of this word.

 : Why don't you look it up in the dictionary?

 : 我不知道這個字的意義。

 : 你為什麼不查字典呢？

補充

look up = consult = refer to

▶▶ lose sb.'s marbles 瘋了

解說

做了些很蠢的事情。

 : I think I am going to break up with Stacy.

 : Have you lost your marbles? Stacy is the hottest girl on school.

 : 我想我會跟史黛西分手。

 : 你瘋了嗎？史黛西是學校最漂亮的女生。

補充

lose sb.'s marbles = go crazy = lose sb.'s mind

▶▶ make a crack about 取笑

：Mom, I want to start choosing my own school clothes.

：Did someone make a crack about your outfit again?

> ：媽媽，我想要開始自己選擇校服。
> ：有人再次取笑你的服裝了嗎？

▶▶ make oneself useful 做點有用的事

解說

讓某人做些有價值的事情。

：Why don't you make yourself useful and give me a hand in the backyard?

：I am trying to watch the football game. It'll be over in one hour, and then I'll help you.

A: 你為什麼不做點有用的事,來後院幫我呢?

B: 我在看足球比賽,它在一小時後會結束,然後我再去幫你。

▶▶ mark down 記下

A: I was in my seat before the bell rang.

B: Nonetheless, I didn't see you, so I marked you down as being late.

A: 鈴聲前我就在位子上了。

B: 但是,我沒看到你,所以我登記你為遲到。

▶▶ mess with 招惹

指挑釁。

A: I have noticed that something has been bothering Peter lately.

B : He told me there is a bully at school that has been messing with him.

A : 我已經注意到，最近有些事情一直困擾著彼得。

B : 他告訴我，學校有位惡霸一直招惹他。

▶▶ **Mickey Mouse** 無關緊要的

A : I'm sick of working on this Mickey Mouse project.

B : For sure. It's not challenging at all.

A : 我厭倦做這無關緊要的計畫。

B : 沒錯，一點挑戰性也沒有。

▶▶ **mint condition** 完好無損

A : Are you trying to play me for a fool? I know damn well these baseball cards are not worth that much.

B : These are mint condition Rookie cards. I thought I was giving you a deal.

：你想玩弄我嗎？我很清楚這些棒球卡不值那麼多錢。

：這些是完好無損的新人卡，我想我給了你一個很好的價錢。

補充

damn well 無疑地，肯定地。

▶▶ **no end in sight** 短期內無法停止

解說

強調事情還會持續下去。

：Do you think we can ever stop destructing the ozone layer?

：As long as there is still a dependency on the combustion of fossil fuels, there will be no end in sight.

：你認為我們能有停止破壞臭氧層的一天嗎？

：只要還依賴石化燃料燃燒，短期內將無法停止。

▶▶ no longer 不再

A : I wanted to see War of the Worlds, but it is no longer playing at the theatre.

B : You can wait for the movie to come out on DVD and rent it then.

> **A** : 我想要看世界大戰,但它已不再在電影院裡播放了。
>
> **B** : 你可以等待這部電影的 DVD 上市,然後租來看。

▶▶ not any more 不再

A : I heard you are not with your girlfriend any more.

B : We broke up last Saturday.

> **A** : 我聽說你不再跟你女友在一起。
>
> **B** : 我們上星期六分手了。

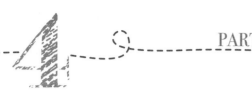

nothing of the kind 一點兒都不像

指毫無類似處，一點兒都不像。

A: I heard Bobby cheated on his test.

B: That cannot be true. He's nothing of the kind.

A: 我聽說鮑比在考試中作弊。

B: 那不可能是真的，他一點兒都不像會作弊的人。

odds and ends 隻字片語

一般指零碎小東西，而用在寫論文的情境中，指隻字片語。

A: Have you completed your thesis?

B: Just touching up on some odds and ends.

A: 你完成你的論文了嗎？

B: 正在修飾一些隻字片語。

▶▶ on sb.'s account 為了某人的緣故

A: Did you join the softball team on my account?

B: No, I joined it because I thought it would be fun.

> **A**: 你是為了我而加入壘球隊嗎?
>
> **B**: 不,我加入是因為我想打壘球會很有趣。

▶▶ one's primary concern
最關心的(事情)

A: Jeff cares more about his nice house and fancy car, than he cares about his friends and family.

B: Ever since he won the lottery, his primary concern has only been money. He doesn't care about anyone anymore.

> **A**: 傑夫較關心他的漂亮房子和高級汽車,而不關心他的朋友和家人。
>
> **B**: 自從他中了樂透後,他最關心的事情只有錢,不再關心任何人。

PART

▶▶ orientation session 新生座談會

就是新生訓練。

A : I heard new students have to attend an orientation session, or they'll not be able to register for classes.

B : Lucky for us, we are not new students.

A : 我聽說新生必須參加新生座談會,否則他們將不能選課。

B : 我們很幸運,我們不是新生。

▶▶ pin down 阻止

使受約束,而動彈不得。

A : The boy is acting up again.

B : Yeah. I'll have to pin him down immediately before he hurts someone.

298

A' : 這小孩又在搗蛋。

B' : 是啊,在他傷到別人之前,我得立刻阻止他。

▶▶ put it mildly 說得婉轉些

put = say 說;mildly 溫和地,強調要說的好聽一點。

A' : What do you think of Professor Vincent Kim's lecture?

B' : To put it mildly, his lectures are boring and un-fulfilling.

A' : 你認為金文森教授的課如何?

B' : 說得婉轉些,他的課很無聊也缺乏成就感。

▶▶ pick up 接收

用在電子產品的收訊或收聽。

A : My stereo can't seem to pick up any frequencies.

B : Why don't you take it in for repair?

A : 我的立體音響似乎不能收到任何頻率。

B : 你為什麼不拿去送修呢？

▶▶ **run for** 競選

A : I heard you want to run for the leader of student government.

B : You bet. Will you vote for me?

A : 我聽說你想要競選學生會主席。

B : 沒錯，你會投給我嗎？

▶▶ **scratch the surface** 只做了粗淺的研究

指研究只觸及表面，沒有深度與全面性。

A : You have found out a lot about the pollution's effects on the environment.

B : Actually, I've only scratched the surface.

A : 你已發現了許多汙染對環境造成的後果。

B : 事實上，我只做了粗淺的研究。

▶▶ **sky-high** 很高

用在形容價錢很高。

A : I heard you had a car crash last week. Were you all right?

B : Fortunately, no one was hurt, but my insurance rates will be sky-high.

A : 我聽說你上週發生車禍，你沒事吧？

B : 很幸運，沒有人受傷，但是我的保險費率會變得很高。

▶▶ smoke like a chimney 菸癮大

A: Your new roommate seems pretty friendly. How do you like him?

B: He's cool, but he smokes like a chimney, and stinks up the house.

A: 你的新室友看起來挺友善，你覺得他怎麼樣呢？

B: 他很優秀，但是他菸癮大，把房間燻得很臭。

▶▶ someone else 另外一個人

指其他人或別人。

A: You remind me of someone else I used to know.

B: Why do you say that?

A: 你使我想起了從前認識的一個人。

B: 你為什麼這樣說呢？

▶▶ steer clear of 不接觸

強調要避開某事。

A : It is hard to steer clear of drugs in high school.

B : Just choose your friends carefully, and you shouldn't have a problem.

A : 在高中時代不接觸毒品是很困難的。

B : 小心選擇你的朋友，你就不會惹上問題。

補充

steer clear of = stay clear of = keep clear of

▶▶ take care of 照顧

A : Ok, we'll be back in two weeks. Call me if you need anything at all.

B : Don't worry. I'll take good care of your puppy.

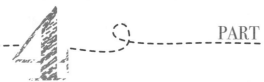

A： 好的，我們在兩週後回來，如果你需要任何東西，打電話給我。

B： 不要擔心，我會好好照顧你的小狗。

▶▶ the birds and bees 性基礎知識

直譯為「鳥和蜜蜂」，引申為「性基礎知識」、「基本性教育」或「兩性關係」。

A： My daughter is awfully shy of talking about the birds and bees.

B： I used to be that way when I was her age.

A： 我女兒在談論性基礎知識十分害羞。

B： 我像她這年紀時，我也是這樣。

▶▶ **the call of nature** 上廁所

直譯為「自然的呼喚」，引申為「上廁所」。

A : Where are you rushing off to?

B : I need to answer the call of nature.

A : 你急著要去哪裡？
B : 我想上廁所。

the call of nature = nature's call = go to see a man about a dog

▶▶ **the picture of** 是…的化身

A : Have you seen Alina lately? I heard she is under the weather.

B : Really? I just saw her, and she looked in the picture of health.

A : 你最近有見到艾琳娜嗎？我聽說她身體不舒服。
B : 真的嗎？我剛看見她，而她看起來很健康。

補充

in the picture of health 健康的化身，表示很健康。

▶▶ the same to 一樣

A: What do you think about politicians?

B: They're all the same to me.

A: 你認為政治家怎麼樣呢？

B: 他們對我來說都一樣。

▶▶ tie up loose ends 處理瑣碎問題

解說

強調未能結束的部分。

A: I am still trying to tie up loose ends with my ex-girlfriend.

B: Don't worry about it. Soon you will end everything and begin again.

A：我還在處理和我前任女朋友之間的瑣碎問題。

B：不要為這事發愁，你很快就會結束一切重新開始。

▶▶ trip up 絆倒

A：Mary tripped up the stairs when entering the stage.

B：Luckily, she didn't get hurt.

A：進入舞臺時，瑪麗被樓梯絆倒了。

B：很幸運，她沒有受傷。

▶▶ turn-off 倒盡胃口

指倒盡胃口的東西。

A：Girls who smoke are a turn-off.

B：Then I guess you won't be interested in Marissa.

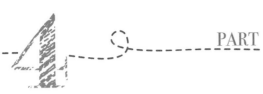

A：抽菸的女孩讓我倒盡胃口。

B：那麼我想你不會對瑪麗莎有興趣。

▶▶ turn the clock back 時光倒流

A：Lately, I often think back to the good old days.

B：Me, too. I wish we could turn the clock back.

A：最近，我常回憶昔日美好時光。

B：我也是，我希望我們能讓時光倒流。

▶▶ whacked out 精神完全失常

指完全瘋掉了。

A：Ever since Jenny started hanging out with those girls, she's been whacked out.

B：She really needs to stop doing drugs. I always thought she had a lot of potential.

PART

A：自從珍妮開始跟那些女孩在一起後，她精神完全失常了。

B：她真的需要停止吸毒，我一直認為她有許多潛力。

▶▶ **with a bang** 非常成功

解 說

直譯為「砰地一聲」，引申為「非常成功」或「大受歡迎」。

A：The semester has started out with a bang. I got all of the classes I wanted, and met up with many old friends.

B：Great, now you only need to pay attention in class.

A：這學期一開始就非常順利，我修到了所有我想要的課程，也遇到許多老朋友。

B：太好了，現在你只需要專心上課。

meet up with 遇到。

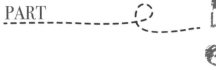

第 **5** 單元

常用短語

PART

▶▶ After you. 你先

A: Do you want to make a presentation first?

B: No, please, after you.

> **A**: 你想第一個做簡報嗎？
> **B**: 不，你先請。

▶▶ All talk, no action. 光說不做

A: Jack promised to help me install an anti-virus software on my computer today.

B: Jack is all talk, no action. I wouldn't be surprised if he didn't even show up.

> **A**: 傑克今天答應幫我在電腦上安裝一套防毒軟體。
> **B**: 傑克光說不做，即使他都沒有出現，我也不會感到意外。

▶▶ Are you kidding? 你是在開玩笑吧

A : The house rent may go up again.

B : Are you kidding? I have no spare money to pay for it.

A : 房租可能再漲。

B : 你是在開玩笑吧？我沒有多餘的錢付房租了。

▶▶ Be my guest. 請自便

有「別客氣」的意思。

A : May I look at your album?

B : Be my guest.

A : 我可以看你的相簿嗎？

B : 請自便。

Be quiet. 安靜

 : Be quiet, please. The baby is asleep.

B : Sorry, I'll go out right now.

> A : 請安靜，嬰兒在睡覺。
>
> B : 抱歉，我立刻出去。

Beats me. 考倒我了

有「不知道」的意思。

A : Do you know why the dinosaurs became extinct?

B : Beats me. I'm not interested in paleontology.

> A : 你知道為什麼恐龍會絕種嗎？
>
> B : 考倒我了，我對古生物學不感興趣。

PART

beats me = I don't know

▶▶ Beauty is only skin deep.
美貌只是表象

A: Beauty is only skin deep.

B: But most people care a lot about their appearance.

> **A:** 美貌只是表象。
>
> **B:** 但是大部份的人非常在意自己的外表。

▶▶ Believe it or not! 信不信由你

A: Believe it or not! I won the lottery.

B: Is that true?

> **A:** 信不信由你！我中了樂透。
>
> **B:** 是真的嗎？

Better late than never.

遲做總比不做好

A : I'm sorry I'm late. I will get on with my work now.

B : Better late than never.

> **A** : 抱歉我遲到了,我現在會開始做我的工作。
>
> **B** : 遲做總比不做好。

Break a leg! 祝你好運

不是斷了一條腿,而是西方人以幽默的話語來祝福別人好運。

A : We will be performing the play on the stage to-morrow.

B : Break a leg!

> **A** : 我們明天會在舞臺上表演話劇。
>
> **B** : 祝你好運!

▶▶ Bring it on. 放馬過來吧

表示不害怕。

A : I challenge you to a game of chess.

B : Bring it on.

A : 我向你挑戰下西洋棋。

B : 放馬過來吧。

▶▶ Business is business. 公事公辦

A : Could you please not give me the ticket?

B : Business is business.

A : 請你不要開罰單給我好嗎？

B : 公事公辦。

PART

►► By all means. 當然可以

A : May I borrow the compact disc handbook?

B : By all means. When will you return it?

> **A** : 我可以借光碟機手冊嗎？
>
> **B** : 當然可以，你什麼時候要歸還呢？

►► Come again? 再說一遍

A : I am going to propose marriage to your sister.

B : Come again? I can't hear you.

> **A** : 我要向你妹妹求婚。
>
> **B** : 再說一遍？我聽不清楚。

目前英文「再說一遍」的客氣委婉表達方式有：Pardon me? 或 Could you say that again?

▶▶ Count me in. 算我一份

A : I will go to the concert tomorrow.

B : Count me in.

> **A** : 明天我會去參加音樂會。
>
> **B** : 算我一份。

▶▶ Count me out. 別把我算在內

A : We're going out for dinner tonight. Would you want to join us?

B : I'm busy. Count me out.

> **A** : 今晚我們要外出吃晚餐,你想和我們一起去嗎?
>
> **B** : 我在忙,別把我算在內。

▶▶ Cut it out! 別鬧了

A : Look at me! Do I look like a gorilla?

B : Cut it out! I've had enough of your silly behavior.

A: 看看我！我有像一隻猩猩嗎？

B: 別鬧了！我已經受夠你的愚蠢行為。

▶▶ Do I make myself clear?
你聽明白了嗎

此句含有警告的意味，用在上對下發生爭吵時。

A: You are not to go out, until your chores are finished. Do I make myself clear?

B: Yes, daddy. I'm crystal clear.

A: 在你的家務事做完之前，你不准出去，聽明白了嗎？

B: 是的，爸爸，我十分清楚。

▶▶ Do you have the time? 現在幾點了

A: Do you have the time?

B : Sorry, I didn't bring my watch today.

A : 現在幾點了？
B : 抱歉，我今天沒帶手錶。

▶▶ Do you have time? 你有空嗎

A : I'd like to get together and talk tonight. Do you have time?

B : I know a cool place down the street where we can go.

A : 我今晚想要跟你聚一聚聊聊天，你有空嗎？
B : 我知道沿著這條街有一個好地點，我們可以去那裡。

▶▶ Don't be a stranger. 保持聯絡

直譯「不要做陌生人」，為邀請某人來訪的告別語，希望彼此間不要太疏遠。

A : It was nice seeing you again, and I'm glad everything is well. Don't be a stranger, and stop by more often.

B : I've just been so busy with work lately. I'll make an effort to come over and visit more.

A : 很高興再次見到你,而我很高興你一切都很好,保持聯絡,有空經常來訪。

B : 我最近工作很忙,我會盡力常過來看你的。

補充

make an effort 努力,盡力。

▶▶ Don't be shy. 別害羞

A : Don't be shy. Please introduce yourselves.

B : I'm shy of speaking in public.

A : 別害羞,請你自我介紹一下。

B : 我怯於在公眾面前講話。

▶▶ Don't count on me. 別指望我

A : Can you give me a lift to school?

B : Don't count on me.

> **A** : 你能讓我搭便車到學校嗎？
>
> **B** : 別指望我。

▶▶ Don't get me wrong. 請別誤解我

A : I don't think you like the movie.

B : Don't get me wrong. I'd like to watch it but I'm preparing for the exam.

> **A** : 我想你不喜歡看這部電影。
>
> **B** : 請別誤解我，我喜歡看，但是我正在準備考試。

▶▶ Don't give me the runaround.
不要拿話搪塞我

A : Sorry, I've just lost my purse and I don't have any money to pay you.

PART

B : Don't give me the runaround. Just tell me you don't have the money.

A : 對不起，我剛遺失錢包，我沒有錢付給你。
B : 不要拿話搪塞我，告訴我你沒錢就行了。

▶▶ Don't let me down. 別讓我失望

A : I don't have much confidence in the finals.

B : Cheer up! Don't let me down.

A : 我對期末考沒有多少信心。
B : 振作一點！別讓我失望。

▶▶ Don't look at me. 別看我

通常表示不同意。

A : Shouldn't someone walk the dog?

B : Don't look at me.

324

A : 是不是應該有人帶狗去散步呢？

B : 別看我，我才不去。

▶▶ Enjoy yourself. 祝你玩得開心

A : I will leave the office and go on holiday tomorrow.

B : Enjoy yourself.

A : 明天我會離開辦公室去度假。

B : 祝你玩得開心。

▶▶ Every Jack has his Jill.
每個男人都會找到適合他的女人

A : What does the love story remind you of ?

B : Every Jack has his Jill.

A : 這個愛情故事使你想到什麼呢？

B : 每個男人都會找到適合他的女人。

▶▶ Far from it! 還差得遠呢

A : I heard you moved into your new house. Have you decorated it yet?

B : Far from it! I haven't bought any furniture yet.

> **A** : 我聽說你搬進了你的新房子，你裝潢了嗎？
>
> **B** : 還差得遠呢！我還沒買任何家具。

▶▶ First things first. 最重要的事情先做

A : How shall we begin the project?

B : First things first. Let's assign roles to everyone first.

> **A** : 我們如何開始這計畫？
>
> **B** : 最重要的事情先做，讓我們先分配每人的角色。

▶▶ Follow me. 跟我走

A : Excuse me. Could you tell me where the new sculpture exhibit is?

B：Follow me. I am going that way now.

A：對不起，你能告訴我這新雕塑展覽會在哪裡嗎？
B：跟我走，我正要去那邊。

▶▶ For sure. 沒錯

常用來表達強烈肯定。

A：I can't believe how hot it is today.

B：For sure. Let's go swimming.

A：我不敢相信今天天氣這麼熱。
B：沒錯，讓我們去游泳吧。

▶▶ Forget it! 算了吧

A：I'm sorry. I've soiled your book.

B：Forget it!

A：對不起，我弄髒你的書。

B：算了吧！

▶▶ Get real. 說真的

A：I am going to school to become a brain surgeon.

B：Get real. I wouldn't want you operating on me.

A：我去上學是為了成為一位腦部外科醫生。

B：說真的，我可不希望你幫我動手術。

補充

operate on 幫…動手術。

▶▶ Got the time? 現在幾點了

解說

此片語來自 Have you got the time? 的縮寫。

A：Got the time?

B : It's a quarter past ten.

A : 幾點了？

B : 現在是十點一刻。

Got the time? = What time is it? = What's the time? = What time do you have?

▶▶ Good thing. 幸好

A : I feel like I didn't pass the pop quiz yesterday.

B : Good thing. It wasn't the midterm.

A : 我感覺我昨天沒有通過隨堂測驗。

B : 幸好，它不是期中考。

▶▶ Great idea. 好主意

A : How about if we go to the mall instead?

B : Great idea.

Ａ：如果我們改成去購物中心如何？

Ｂ：好主意。

▶▶ Great minds think alike.
英雄所見略同

Ａ：As for dropping French, I second you.

Ｂ：Great minds think alike.

Ａ：至於要退選法文課，我支持你。

Ｂ：英雄所見略同。

▶▶ Have you got a light? 你有火嗎

Ａ：Hey, have you got a light?

Ｂ：No, I don't smoke.

Ａ：嗨，你有火嗎？

Ｂ：沒有，我不抽菸。

PART

▶▶ He hasn't been himself. 他心不在焉

是指他的心在某處。

A: Ever since Mary broke up with Bob, he hasn't been himself.

B: I am sure as soon as he meets another girl, he'll snap out of it.

A: 自從瑪麗跟鮑伯分手後,他心不在焉。

B: 我確信一旦他遇到另一個女孩,他馬上就會振作起來。

▶▶ Here's the deal. 事情是這樣的

A: Come on, man. I'm 25 years old.

B: Here's the deal. Without ID to prove you're over 21, you're not coming into this bar.

A: 拜託,老兄,我25歲了。

B: 事情是這樣的,沒有身分證證明你超過21歲,你不能進入這酒吧。

331

PART

▶▶ Hurry up. 快一點

A: Hurry up, Michael. We're going to be late for the show.

B: Can you please wait for me to comb my hair?

> **A:** 快一點,麥克,我們看表演就要遲到了。
>
> **B:** 你可以等我梳個頭髮嗎?

▶▶ I beg your pardon? 請你再說一遍

A: I heard Duke is off to the golf course.

B: I beg your pardon?

> **A:** 我聽說杜克要去高爾夫球場。
>
> **B:** 請你再說一遍?

▶▶ I can't follow you. 我不懂你說的

A: Do you understand me?

B: I am sorry. I can't follow you.

A : 你懂我的意思嗎？

B : 抱歉，我不懂你說的。

▶▶ I have no choice. 我別無選擇

A : Why did you buy that pair of slippers?

B : I have no choice they were a gift.

A : 你為什麼買這雙拖鞋呢？

B : 我別無選擇，因為它是贈品。

▶▶ I couldn't agree more. 我非常同意

A : I'll take care of the food, if you bring the drinks to the party.

B : I couldn't agree more. I'll pick up some beer on the way.

A : 如果你帶飲料來參加宴會，我就會負責食物的部分。

B : 我非常同意，我會在路上買些啤酒。

▶▶ I'm in a hurry. 我在趕時間

A: We can take a shortcut to the airport.

B: That's great. I'm in a hurry.

A: 我們可以抄近路到機場。
B: 太好了，我在趕時間。

▶▶ I'm on your side. 我支持你

A: I am planning to run for student representative.

B: Go for it. I'm on your side.

A: 我計畫競選學生代表。
B: 加油，我支持你。

▶▶ I'm speechless. 我說不出話來

因驚訝而不知要說什麼。

A : Hey, mom. I just asked Nancy to marry me. So, what do you say?

B : I don't know what to say. I'm speechless.

A : 嗨！媽媽，我剛向薾西求婚，所以妳覺得呢？
B : 我不知道我要說什麼，我說不出話來。

▶▶ I'm stuffed. 我吃飽了

A : The food is delicious. Have some more, please.

B : No, thanks. I'm stuffed.

A : 食物很好吃，請多吃一點。
B : 不，謝謝，我很飽了。

▶▶ I see. 我知道

A : You should take careful notes next time.

B : I see. Thank you.

A : 你下次應該認真記筆記。

B : 我知道,謝謝你。

▶▶ I think so. 我也這麼想

A : I'm very hungry. I think we should go out for dinner soon.

B : I think so.

A : 我很餓,我想我們應該儘快外出吃晚餐。

B : 我也這麼想。

▶▶ Is that your story? 那是你的理由嗎

A : My dog ate my homework.

B : Is that your story? I'm afraid that's not a valid excuse.

A : 我的狗吃下了我的回家作業。

B : 那是你的理由嗎?恐怕那不是一個正當理由。

▶▶ It's a piece of cake. 小事一樁

直譯為「這是一片蛋糕」，引申為像吃蛋糕一樣容易。

A : Thank you for helping me to find a job.

B : Don't mention it. It's a piece of cake.

A : 謝謝你幫我找到一份工作。

B : 不客氣，小事一樁。

▶▶ It's up to you. 由你決定

A : May I invite Mary to the reception?

B : It's up to you.

A : 我可以邀請瑪麗參加招待會嗎？

B : 由你決定。

PART

▶▶ Join the club. 同病相憐

 解說

歡迎加入俱樂部，引申為同病相憐。

> **A**: I am sick of living paycheck to paycheck.
>
> **B**: Join the club! I can barely afford to eat out at McDonald's.

> **A**: 我厭倦當個月光族。
>
> **B**: 同病相憐！我幾乎沒錢外出吃麥當勞了。

補充

join the club = join the party

▶▶ Let's move it! 快一點

> **A**: We're going to be late for school. Let's move it!
>
> **B**: Let me go to the bathroom first.

> **A**: 我們上學要遲到了，快一點！
>
> **B**: 讓我先進浴室吧。

▶▶ Keep in touch. 保持聯絡

A : I have to go home. Bye-bye.

B : See you later. Keep in touch.

A : 我要回家了,再見。

B : 再見,保持聯絡。

▶▶ Let's get this show on the road.
我們開始吧

A : Okay, students. Let's get this show on the road. We only have 45 minutes to hear all of your presentations.

B : I hope there isn't enough time left to hear ours.

A : 好的,學生們,讓我們開始吧,我們只有45分鐘來聽你們所有人的簡報。

B : 我希望沒有足夠的時間來聽我們的簡報。

補充

Let's get this show on the road. = Let's start it. = Let's go

---

 Let me see. 讓我想一想

解說

Let me see 有另一意思是「讓我看一看」。

A : What is the price of new clothes?

B : Well, let me see.

A : 這新衣服的價錢是多少？
B : 嗯，讓我想一想。

 Make it easy on you. 放你一馬

A : Since students have been so attentive all se-mester, I'll make it easy on you, when it's time for the final.

B : I knew our hard work would pay off.

A：既然學生整學期都很專心，在期末考時，我會放你們一馬。

B：我知道我們努力用功是值得的。

Make up your mind. 做個決定吧

A：There are so many choices, but I don't know which one to choose.

B：Make up your mind. There is no time to waste.

A：有很多的選擇，但是我不知道該選哪一個。

B：做個決定吧，不能再浪費時間了。

Never mind. 沒關係

A：Sorry, I can't sing the English song.

B：Never mind. I can teach you.

 ：對不起，我不會唱英文歌。

B ：沒關係，我可以教你。

▶▶ No kidding. 沒錯

解說

用在附和別人的意見時，解釋為「沒錯、真的、對啊」，有 of course 的意思。

A ：I heard that Harvard is a difficult school to get in to.

B ：No kidding.

A ：我聽說哈佛大學是很難進入的學校。

B ：沒錯。

▶▶ No pain, no gain.
沒有付出，就沒有收穫

A ：To be an actor is to pay a price.

B : After all, no pain, no gain.

A : 要成為演員是要付出代價。

B : 畢竟，沒有付出，就沒有收穫。

▶▶ No sweat. 沒問題

A : Do you think you'd be able to take your car tomorrow?

B : No sweat.

A : 你想明天能開你的車嗎？

B : 沒問題。

no sweat = no problem

▶▶ Right back at you. 謝謝，我也是

也可譯為「彼此彼此」。

A : I'll take you as one of my best friends.

B : Right back at you.

> **A** : 我把你當作我最好的朋友之一。
> **B** : 謝謝，我也是。

►► Say no more. 別再說了

A : Say no more. What do you want to buy?

B : I want to buy a tablet.

> **A** : 別再說了，你想買什麼？
> **B** : 我想買一台平板電腦。

►► Search me. 我不知道

A : What do you want to buy her for her birthday party?

B : Search me. Any ideas?

A : 你想要為她的生日宴會買什麼呢？

B : 我不知道，有任何主意嗎？

▶▶ Shame on you. 你真丟臉

A : Shame on you. I see you dropping litter on the floor.

B : I'm sorry. I'll pick it up right now.

A : 你真丟臉，我看見你亂丟垃圾在地板上。

B : 抱歉，我立刻撿起來。

▶▶ So far, so good. 目前一切順利

A : What about your thesis?

B : So far, so good.

A : 你的論文如何呢？

B : 目前一切順利。

▶▶ Speak of the devil! 說曹操，曹操到

A : Speak of the devil! We were just talking about you.

B : All good, I hope.

A : 說曹操，曹操到！我們正在談論你。
B : 希望都是說我的好話。

Speak of the devil! = Speak of angels, and you will hear their wings

▶▶ Spit it out. 快說吧

A : Spit it out. What do you want to borrow?

B : I want to borrow your notes.

A : 快說吧，你想要借什麼？
B : 我想要借你的筆記。

▶▶ Stop kicking yourself. 不要自責

A : I'm stupid. I should have known not to trust Kevin with my car.

B : Stop kicking yourself. You didn't know he had no driver's license.

A : 我很笨,我早該知道不要把車交給凱文。

B : 不要自責,你不知道他沒有駕駛執照。

start kicking yourself 開始自責。

▶▶ Sure thing. 那是一定的

解說

強調肯定,是 sure 的加強語氣。

A : Do you need a ride?

B : Sure thing.

A : 你要搭便車嗎?

B : 那是一定的。

Take care. 保重

A : I have to go. See you.

B : Ok. Take care, please.

> **A** : 我必須走了，再見。
> **B** : 好的，請保重。

Take it easy. 別緊張

A : I lost my pet. Can you help me?

B : Take it easy and say it slowly.

> **A** : 我遺失了我的寵物，你能幫忙我嗎？
> **B** : 別緊張，慢慢說。

The more, the merrier. 人越多越開心

A : May I bring two friends to your party tonight?

B : The more, the merrier.

A : 我今晚可以帶兩位朋友來參加你的宴會嗎？

B : 人越多越開心。

▶▶ Time is running out. 時間快到了

指時間不多了。

A : Have you submitted your college applications yet? If not, you'd better hurry, because time is running out.

B : I am almost finished with them. I should be able to meet the deadline.

A : 你有繳交你的大學申請表嗎？如果沒有，你最好快點，因為時間快到了。

B : 我差不多快寫完了，我應該可以在截止日期之前完成。

▶▶ Time is up. 時間到了

A : Time is up. Hand in your paper, please.

B : Oops! I failed to complete the last question.

A : 時間到了，請交出試卷。
B : 糟糕！我還沒有寫完最後一個問題。

▶▶ That depends. 那要看情況

A : Can you give me a discount?

B : Well, that depends.

A : 你能給我打折嗎？
B : 嗯，那要看情況。

▶▶ That suits me. 那正適合我

A : I heard the part-time job is on-campus and two hours per day.

B : That suits me.

> **A**：我聽說這兼職工作是在校內，而且每天工作兩小時。
>
> **B**：那正適合我。

▶▶ That makes two of us. 英雄所見略同

> 指強調同意，有「我也一樣」或「我也是」的意思。

> **A**：The bright day makes me feel better.
>
> **B**：That makes two of us.

> **A**：天氣晴朗讓我感到心情特別好。
>
> **B**：英雄所見略同。

▶▶ That was too close. 真是好險

> **A**：We were almost caught cutting class by the principal.
>
> **B**：That was too close. We need to be more careful next time.

A : 我們翹課差一點被校長抓到。

B : 真是好險，下次我們要更小心一點。

▶▶ That's easier said than done.
說得容易做起來難

A : Please forget me.

B : That's easier said than done.

A : 請忘了我吧。

B : 說得容易做起來難。

▶▶ Time is money. 時間就是金錢

A : Please don't waste my time.

B : Time is money, I know.

A : 請不要浪費我的時間。

B : 我知道，時間就是金錢。

PART

▶▶ Try again. 再試試

A: I called Peter, but the line is busy.

B: Wait a minute. Try again, please.

> **A**: 我打電話給彼得，但是電話忙線中。
>
> **B**: 等一下，請再試試。

▶▶ Watch your step. 小心走路

強調小心謹慎。

A: The rain is heavy. And I have to go home.

B: Please watch your step. The road is slippery.

> **A**: 雨下很大，而我必須回家。
>
> **B**: 請小心走路，路面很滑。

▶▶ What a coincidence! 真巧

A : I work for ASU.

B : What a coincidence! Me, too.

> A : 我在 ASU 工作。
>
> B : 真巧！我也是。

▶▶ What a good deal! 真便宜

A : The sneakers are 500 dollars after the discount.

B : What a good deal!

> A : 運動鞋打折後是500美元。
>
> B : 真便宜！

▶▶ What a pity. 真可惜

A : The film has an exciting plot.

B : What a pity. It didn't win any awards.

A : 這部電影有吸引人的情節。

B : 真可惜，它沒有贏得任何獎項。

What a pity. = What a shame

▶▶ ## What a shame. 真可惜

A : I haven't been to the conference.

B : What a shame. You missed a good chance.

A : 我沒有去參加研討會。

B : 真可惜，你失去一個好機會。

▶▶ ## What did you do for a living?
你是做什麼為生

A : What did you do for a living before joining the Peace Corps?

B : I used to be a police officer in New York.

 ：在進入和平工作團前，你是做什麼為生呢？

B：我過去在紐約當警官。

▶▶ What do you say?

你的意思是怎麼樣呢

解說

用在徵求別人意見時使用。

A：What do you say we go out for ice-cream after dinner?

B：Sure, as long as you're buying.

A：晚飯後，我們外出吃冰淇淋，你的意思是怎麼樣呢？

B：當然可以，只要是你請客。

▶▶ Whatever you say 聽你的

解說

就是你怎麼說就怎麼辦，也就是你說的算。

A : You'd better bring home a good report card next semester, or you'll be grounded.

B : Whatever you say, dad.

A : 你下學期最好要帶優秀的成績單回家,否則你就會被禁足。

B : 爸爸,聽你的。

▶▶ Who's with me? 你要加入嗎

指問誰願意加入我的行列。

A : I say we organize our own club. Who's with me?

B : No, thanks. I'm in enough clubs already.

A : 我說我們來組自己的社團,你要加入嗎?

B : 不,謝謝,我已經參加很多社團了。

此短語在不同的情境有不同的意思,如「誰和我一起去呢?」、「你要加入嗎?」、「你們同意嗎?」、「誰支持我呢?」等。

▶▶ Well done. 做得很好

A: I'm finally done. I put a lot of time into it.

B: Well done. I think the paper will get top marks.

A: 我終於做完了,我花了很多時間。

B: 做得很好,我想這份報告會得到高分的。

▶▶ With all due respect. 恕我直言

直譯「以對你該有的尊敬」,引申為不同意某人的意見或看法,但是還是很尊重他,在翻譯上一般都翻做「我冒昧地說一句」或「恕我直言」。

A: I think I should be the team captain.

B: With all due respect, I don't believe you have the necessary experience and skill to get the position.

A: 我想我應該當球隊隊長。

B: 恕我直言,我不覺得你具備必要的經驗和技術能勝任這職位。

PART

Wonders never cease!
驚奇的事永遠不停歇

A：I passed the final exam.

B：Wonders never cease!

> **A**：我通過了期末考試。
> **B**：驚奇的事永遠不停歇！

You are telling me!
這還用你說，我知道

強調我早就知道了，用在表示同意。

A：Phew! That was a close call. I almost got caught by the teacher.

B：You're telling me.

> **A**：喲！真險啊，我差點被老師抓到了。
> **B**：這還用你說，我知道！

▶▶ # You bet. 你說的沒錯

是肯定用語，一般翻譯為「當然」、「眞的」、「的確」、「你說得沒錯」。

A : Do you want to go to the lake this weekend?

B : You bet. I'll bring the booze.

A : 你這個週末想要去湖邊嗎？

B : 你說得沒錯，我會帶酒去。

▶▶ # You can bet your life. 當然可以

A : Could you tell me where the administration building is?

B : You can bet your life. Go down this street and turn left at the last intersection.

A : 你能告訴我行政大樓在哪裡？

B : 當然可以，沿著這條街走，到最後交叉路口左轉。

▶▶ You can make it. 你能做到

A: I hope to have a scholarship this semester.

B: You are considered the best in the school. I believe you can make it.

A: 這學期我希望能獲得獎學金。

B: 全校就你功課最好，我相信你能做到。

▶▶ You have my word. 我向你保證

A: Don't tell the teacher, whatever you do! It's between you and me.

B: You have my word. I won't tell a soul.

A: 無論如何都不要告訴老師！它是我們之間的祕密。

B: 我向你保證，我不會告訴任何人。

▶▶ You matter to me. 你對我很重要

A: Why do you care so much whether or not I do well in school?

B: You matter to me, which is why I hope you do well.

> **A:** 你為什麼很關心我在校的成績好壞呢？
>
> **B:** 你對我很重要，那也是為什麼我希望你表現出色的原因。

do well in 在某方面表現出色。

▶▶ You owe me one. 你欠我一個人情

A: I helped you out last time. You owe me one.

B: I will remember your help forever.

> **A:** 上次我幫助你，你欠我一個人情。
>
> **B:** 我永遠都會記住你的幫助。

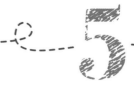

▶▶ You're nuts. 你瘋了

A : I personally do not think Beth is that attractive.

B : You're nuts. Beth is the hottest girl at our school.

A : 我個人認為貝絲不是那麼吸引人。

B : 你瘋了，貝絲在我們學校是最漂亮的。

▶▶ You're pulling my leg. 你在開玩笑

對某人所說的話感到懷疑，而此短語直譯為「你在拉我的腿」，但完全沒有拉我的腿的涵意，其中關鍵片語 pull (sb.'s) leg 為開（某人的）玩笑之意。

A : I think Helen will win the tennis game this year.

B : You're pulling my leg. Have you seen her form recently?

A : 我想今年海倫會贏得網球比賽。

B : 你在開玩笑，你有看到她最近的狀態嗎？

▶▶ You're up. 輪到你

 : You're up next, Bobby. Good luck.

 : Thanks, I hope you like my performance.

 : 鮑比，下一個輪到你了，祝你好運。

 : 謝謝，我希望你喜歡我的表演。

補充

You're up. = It's your turn

國家圖書館出版品預行編目資料

口說校園生活英文片語會話／王仁癸著.--初
版.--臺北市：書泉，2014.08
　面；　公分
ISBN 978-986-121-935-6（平裝附光碟片）
1.英語　2.會話　3.慣用語
805.188　　　　　　　　　　103012699

3AN8

口說校園生活英文片語會話

作　　　者 ― 王仁癸(17.4)

發 行 人 ― 楊榮川

總 編 輯 ― 王翠華

主　　　編 ― 朱曉蘋

責任編輯 ― 吳雨潔

封面設計 ― 吳佳臻

出 版 者 ― 書泉出版社

地　　　址：106台北市大安區和平東路二段339號4樓

電　　　話：(02)2705-5066　　傳　　　真：(02)2706-6100

網　　　址：http://www.wunan.com.tw

電子郵件：shuchuan@shuchuan.com.tw

劃撥帳號：01303853

戶　　　名：書泉出版社

經 銷 商：朝日文化

進退貨地址：新北市中和區橋安街15巷1號7樓

TEL：(02)2249-7714　　FAX：(02)2249-8715

法律顧問　林勝安律師事務所　林勝安律師

出版日期　2014年8月初版一刷

定　　　價　新臺幣450元